Copyright © Claude Dancourt 2014
http://www.claudedancourt.webs.com

ISBN (ebook): 978-0-9880313-5-7
ISBN (hard copy): 978-0-9880313-4-0

Cover Artist: Claude Dancourt
Editor: Lorelei Logsdon

To A., H., and K.
Shall you never be forgotten.

SECOND CHANCES

By

Claude Dancourt

Prologue

The rear lights disappeared slowly into the night as Arthur drove away. Maya wiped the fogging glass to follow the red glow through the falling snow a little longer. This dinner (this *date*, as he insisted calling it) had been Arthur's call. Despite her apprehension at first, it had turned surprisingly comfortable. They had argued only once or twice – a Guinness Book record.

Oh, Arthur did annoy her. He played her nerves like a maestro his fiddle, until she felt ready to explode. If the music would be a mad Caprice from Paganini or an ethereal Celtic ballad, however, she had no clue. And damn him, she was curious to find out.

He confused her. Who was Arthur Pendleton, really? Was he the conceited, dutiful son of a greedy man, with an agenda of his own in their little masquerade? Or, were arrogance and sarcasm just a mask to conceal a more complex, sensitive character?

Some bits of their conversation came back to her mind.

"I still don't understand why you can't simply say no to Robert about his marital ideas instead of all this machination."

Arthur reacted instantly.

"You don't know what it's like to deal with a man who does not consider 'no' as a suitable answer."

She did not; but she could guess well enough. Be successful; be flawless; obey blindly. She'd had her share when she was younger, when she was in high school and Robert still cared about the whereabouts of his goddaughter.

Their waiter presented Arthur with his coffee and left. She watched her companion more closely as he spooned his coffee unnecessarily – his stare fixed on the dark beverage, sailing

away already. Maya refused to let him close up so she teased,
"You could do worse than Isobel. At least she is nice."

After a moment, Arthur looked up. His expression was
mocking again and she dreaded his response.

"You surprise me, Maya. You, of all people, approving of
arranged unions?"

Maya tensed. "I don't—"

"No, of course you don't. You are a romantic at heart."
She frowned.

"If I was that *romantic, I would get caught in this*
masquerade, fall helplessly in love with you, and nurse a
broken heart for the rest of my life."

Arthur laughed and gestured for the bill.

"Fortunately for your tender heart, this has little chance of
happening, right?"

She liked his tone less and less and replied dryly.
"Absolutely."

Maya turned away from the window. Yes, her heart was
safe with Arthur; still, she wondered…

Chapter 1

Some days earlier…

Maya felt bone-tired. She rubbed her eyes once more, but her vision stayed blurred. She was sure she would fall asleep if she dared close her eyes for only a second. She had been up since dawn, going through her list of daily chores, making sure breakfast would be ready for the children and parents alike. Then she had spent the afternoon at the Make-a-Wish ward.

Most of the kids in that part of the house (she refused to call it a hospital) suffered from severe or incurable illnesses. Yet, when she listened to them talking about their wishes, Maya couldn't stop her heart from praying for a miracle.

She remembered little Sally, who had wished to visit Disney World and talk to Mickey Mouse. Two months after travelling back from Florida, the medical treatment had finally started to work on her, and now she was back home.

Maya smiled at the memory. And then there had been Jonathan, who was a soccer fan and wanted to meet with David Beckham. The superstar had invited him to the first England match at the World Cup as his personal guest at the stadium, if only the little boy fought until he could receive a new heart. And he had; Maya had pinned the photo of Jonathan with his hero on her fridge. And Sam, who hated when her brother called her Samantha, but wanted a cat to give to her brother so he would remember her. Lovely little Sam was gone now…

The young woman took off her glasses and pinched her nose to stop the moisture invading her burning eyes. A new patient had arrived the previous week, an eight-year-old boy called Matthew. The orphanage had sent him to the Vallon

Hospital because he refused to eat and often had trouble breathing; they had believed it was serious asthma, but the doctor had finally identified a very rare form of throat cancer. They discovered the tumor very late, thus chemotherapy was not an option. Surgery was costly, with poor chance of success.

The Gerald Finnegan Foundation, named after her father, had funds for these situations where patients didn't have the resources to pay for medical assistance. Yet, when Maya had tried to fill in a form for Matthew's operation, the system had informed her that the foundation account was unavailable. This was strange but the software was temperamental so she tried it a second time. And a third. At the fourth attempt, the system had completely frozen. This was why she was still at her office at one in the morning trying to overcome the computer's irksome behavior.

The program beeped again, announcing another failure, and Maya snorted in frustration. She wanted the form to be completed and in the system as soon as possible; Matthew needed it.

She did not fully understand why she was so drawn to the boy; she wanted to protect him, to keep him safe and feeling loved. Maybe it was her biological clock starting to ticktock. Or maybe it was just because of who she was, the champion of lost causes, as Moira called her. Her sister didn't say that in a bad way. Simply, it was something they didn't have in common, that craving Maya felt to fight for those who could not.

The software finally unlocked, and she managed to access the foundation's bank account. Her jaw dropped. The account was empty. The hundreds of thousands of dollars her father had left and that they had used to build a charity foundation to help children in need of medical help were gone. Impossible. No one but herself, Moira, and their cousin Tristan had authority to use the money. Surely this was another flaw in the system. Maya pressed a key to refresh the data, and her computer froze again.

"Damn!"

"You have the nicest way to welcome late visitors, honey pot."

Maya jumped at the voice. Focused on her task, she had not heard her friend Colin coming into the room.

"What are you doing here, Colin?"

"Gavin needed a lift."

She smiled at the soft inflexion in his voice. Gavin and Colin were still in the honeymoon phase of their relationship, totally smitten with each other. It was really sweet. She was glad her friend had finally accepted his homosexuality, after years of self-torture, mostly because he feared his friends' reactions, in particular that of his boss. Arthur represented the archetype of machismo, an arrogant playboy, selfish and shallow to a fault, more interested in looking at his pretty face in a mirror than in the well-being of those around him. But given that he hadn't disowned Colin or fired him (and she had heard he sometimes hung out with Colin and Gavin), at least he seemed to hide some good sense in that inflated head of his.

Maya snorted again. She had more important things to do than waste energy thinking about Arthur.

Colin bent over her shoulder to check her computer.

"What are you doing?"

"I wanted to fill in a form for Matthew with the Foundation, but the system is not cooperating tonight. It had a crazy warning about the account being empty!"

The young man punched a couple of keys. The computer reacted at once, which annoyed her very much. She had been at it for hours …

"It's not empty, it's frozen. Wait a minute."

Maya watched while Colin looked for more details.

"This line says the account is frozen."

"What?"

She didn't understand. Who had ordered the freeze of the funds? Matthew needed the money! Colin shook his head.

"Sorry, there's nothing about it in there."

Maya sighed heavily, defeated.

"I will talk to Moira first thing tomorrow morning. Maybe she knows what the problem is."

Colin squeezed her arm, worried at the tiredness in her voice.

"Do you want me to drive you home?"

"Yes, thanks."

She didn't feel like taking the bus, and if she called for a taxi, it would take hours before getting one. The Christmas season was her favorite time of the year, but it was dreadful for someone who didn't own a car.

Colin helped her with her coat, and she let him escort her through the silent corridors down to the parking lot.

"Are you coming to the Yule Ball this year?"

"No."

He took the hint at once. Her relations with the Pendletons were tense ever since Maya had chosen to take her sister's side in the battle of wills between Moira and Robert. Her father had founded Pendletons & Associates with Robert and his wife Abigail. When her sister, coming of age, had announced her intent to use her inheritance to initiate the Gerald Finnegan Foundation, instead of reinvesting it in the firm, Robert hadn't been pleased, to say the least.

Maya smirked, the effect spoiled by another yawn.

"I didn't receive an invitation anyway."

She pointed a threatening finger toward him before he even opened his mouth.

"And I don't want one! Don't even think about talking to His Majesty about it."

Her friend offered an angelic smile, and put the car into gear.

*

Arthur groaned. The answering machine was blinking, announcing he had seven new messages, and he guessed every one of them was from Emily. The damned girl couldn't understand the meaning of the word 'over'.

She had been more a distraction than anything; and wooing her when that idiot Luke had his eyes on her had been fun. But she had taken his interest a little too seriously, and started talking chapels and kids.

Arthur liked kids. Kids were miniature versions of adults, with more good sense than several grown-ups he knew. He liked chapels too; he had nice memories of some he had visited in France and Italy. However, the association of the two in Emily's mouth had the flavor of commitment, which was definitely not on his Christmas list.

He felt bored. Ever since Colin had found his soul mate in Gavin, an attendant at the Vallon Hospital, he was not the fun he used to be. More than often he was eager to leave at the end of the day, instead of lingering for a drink or a game of pool. Arthur reset the answering machine and then moved to the cupboard to pour himself a scotch, while he went through his notebook.

The Yule Ball was in less than two weeks, and he needed some cute undemanding accessory wrapped around his arm to entertain him, before his father started on again about the responsibilities and duties of the only heir of Pendletons & Associates; responsibilities which included to escort (and eventually propose to) the daughter of some business associate, for an example.

Chapter 2

Moira paced the room in fury.

"There is only one person who has the authority to freeze the account, that's Robert! Father's will states that Pendletons & Associates would manage the account. How dare he!?"

Her sister had been repeating the same thing over and over since Maya had told her about Colin's finding. The beautiful blonde brutally slammed the file she was holding on the desk. Maya jumped. Moira was so temperamental these days ... Her sister started walking the room back and forth again.

"He's going too far. Last month, he asked, no, he *demanded* that his dolt of a son be named to the board along with the three of us, and now this! I will not allow it!"

She grabbed the phone. Maya gently put one hand on her sister's arm.

"Robert will refuse to talk to you. I'll go ..."

Putting the receiver down, Moira looked up at her baby sister.

"Maya ..."

The raven-haired woman smiled bravely.

"Even if he resents me for choosing to work with you, he won't refuse to explain. Please, let me try."

Moira caressed the hand gently holding hers. Maya's godfather's fierce attitude toward them was yet another reason to hate him. Robert had fostered the two sisters after the death of their parents, despite his own grief over his wife's disappearance just months before. He had been like a second father to Maya, treating her like his own daughter. However, when she decided to support Moira's plans for a medical foundation, he started acting with Maya the same way he did with everyone else, including his own son: distant and tyrannical. His apparent change of heart had hurt her deeply.

"Are you sure?"

Maya nodded.

"Yes, he will talk to me. He is my godfather, after all."

"Very well, then. You didn't tell me how you discovered–"

A sharp rap on the door interrupted her and an old man entered the office. Moira signalled him to take a seat but he refused politely. Maya stiffened at once.

"Doctor?"

"Maya, you asked me yesterday to tell you when I received the biopsy results for young Matthew."

Suddenly she felt cold. The doctor continued.

"The tumor is malignant and located in a sensitive area. It grows fast. It's pressing against his esophagus already, and if he is not operated on soon …"

The old man trailed off. Maya swallowed the hard knot that was forming in her throat. "Thank you."

He took his leave, with a quick nod toward the two women. Moira narrowed her dark eyes on her younger sister. The fate of the little boy was affecting her baby sister a lot, and she looked on the verge of crying. She squeezed her hand gently.

"Why don't you call P and A, and ask for a meeting with Robert as soon as possible? Then you'll join Cedric and me for lunch."

Maya bit the inside of her cheek. Cedric was Moira's fiancé. She didn't like the guy very much. However, she had to admit he seemed really in love with Moira, even if his manners sometimes needed a lot of improvement.

"Thanks, but I'm already meeting Tristan."

Moira frowned. Their cousin was hardly a cheer-up since his long-time girlfriend had broken up with him and accepted a more lucrative proposal. The *'lucky'* groom was twice her age. Good riddance, if someone asked her. Yet Maya and he were close, with a common passion for music and lost causes …

"As you wish. Give Tristan my best."

Maya smiled, and exited the room.

*

Maya stepped out of her taxi. Pendletons & Associates' headquarters was located on one of the most elitist streets of the city.

She remembered when the three-story building was a happy sight, because she was eager to run into her godfather's welcoming arms. He used to complain her enthusiastic kisses undermined his authority on the staff. The young woman chuckled bitterly. She certainly was not enthusiastic anymore, and would probably be even less welcome.

A couple was arguing on the steps, the woman pointing a threatening finger toward the man who had his back to Maya. He ran one hand through his blond hair, and the familiar gesture identified him at once.

Maya glanced around, wondering if there was another way to enter the building to avoid passing by Arthur and his latest fling. No such luck.

Resigned, she climbed the steps and quickly moved toward the main door when a hand grabbed her elbow roughly, forcing her to turn.

"Emily, please meet Maya, we …"

"Her?"

A disdainful sneer erupted from the petite brunette in front of Arthur. Maya held up her chin, the mocking tone erasing her urge to escape Arthur's strong grasp. The annoyed blue eyes stopped examining her old coat and the handcrafted red scarf to glance back at his lady-friend.

"I told you before. It's over."

Without another word, Arthur escorted Maya inside the building. As soon as they were out of sight, she freed her arm abruptly. The rebuff amused him and he sneered.

"To what do we owe the pleasure of the prodigal ward's visit?"

"I have to talk to your father."

"Do you have an appointment?"

Maya glanced away. She had called, but of course on hearing her name, Robert's assistant had announced his agenda was full for at least two weeks. Matthew could not wait that long... Arthur's face was unreadable.

"I thought so. Colin!"

The young man poked his head out from behind a door and grinned.

"Yes? Hey Maya, it's good to see you, what are you doing here?"

"Hello, Colin."

Her friend was the first person she was glad to see and she smiled at him sweetly.

"Colin, call Lucy and tell her I'm coming up to see my father."

That was unexpected. Arthur turned to Maya, who tried to hide her surprise behind a mask of indifference.

"Don't get all worked up, I'm just returning the favor after your *'help'* with that idiot outside. I hope you have a good reason to want to see him, I am not in mood for another round of your Finnegan versus Pendleton contest. And take that thing off, it's ugly."

Gratitude vanished under the patronizing tone. Maya shrugged her shoulders, and punched the elevator's button. She was not going to complain if Arthur thought he had to pay some nonexistent debt, but in no way she was going to give him the satisfaction of seeing her smile and bow. What a jerk!

She pitied the poor girl outside, until she recalled the venomous glance the so-called Emily had shot her and the disdain in her voice after Arthur hinted she was the new flavor of the month. Arthur's conquests were generally as vain as he was. Birds of a feather …

The elevator stopped on the third floor. The place hadn't changed that much. The first door they passed by still opened onto the conference room; the second one onto the library.

With Christmas season coming, the tall windows were not enough to light the corridor even at midday, so the wall lamps were adding some golden gleam to the mahogany furniture and the rich colors on the walls. The sight brought a smile, quickly dismissed. The last door was Robert's office.

SECOND CHANCES

Chapter 3

Robert didn't look up when he heard the door. Maya used the extra seconds to appraise him.

He was still fit, with maybe a little more gray in his hair, and more wrinkles on his forehead and around the eyes.

"Arthur, didn't I tell you already not to interrupt me when …"

"Good morning, Robert."

His steel-blue eyes shot up and the middle-aged man leaned back in his chair. Maya could imagine him very well with a crown on his head, comfortably installed on a throne, signing an innocent person's death warrant with a wave of his hand. He refused to acknowledge her polite greeting and turned to his son.

"What is she doing here?"

Maya took one step forward.

"Robert, I've come to talk to you about the freezing of the Gerald Finnegan Foundation account. I don't know why you did that, but there is this boy, Matthew, he needs an operation and—"

She stopped talking as soon as he raised one hand.

"I'm not interested in your tragic tales. I am Gerald's executor and when the banker reported illicit financial trading to me, I had no choice but to freeze the account. Blame your pitiful managing if your protégé is suffering the consequences now, not me."

"What illicit operations?"

Her godfather shook his head in amusement at her genuinely surprised tone.

"I suggest you ask your sister. Now if we are done here …"

"Robert, please"–

"You're a sweet girl, Maya, but you are misguided. I hope you'll come back to your senses before your sister corrupts you completely. Good day."

She wanted to insist but Robert had already returned his full attention to his work. Unwanted tears burned her eyes. He was so unfair.

"I can't believe you're so heartless! He is just a kid! He is going to die if he is not operated on soon, and the Foundation was created for people like him. People, Robert, not pieces of paper to discard as casualties in your ridiculous crusade against my sister!"

"Enough. Arthur, show her out."

The dutiful son she had momentarily forgotten tried to take her arm, but Maya jerked away from his touch.

"Get your hands off me."

She stormed out of the room and rushed down the stairs, where she was sure Arthur would not follow her. The atmosphere of the building, once so cherished, was sickening. She couldn't wait to get out. Maya didn't even stop to talk to Colin when he stepped out of his office to greet her. His question of what was wrong disappeared in the pounding in her head.

Once she reached the street and turned around the corner, Maya stopped fleeing and leaned on the wall. At least the tears were gone. She took deep breaths in order to calm the frantic beat of her heart, and composed herself before she faced Tristan. Her cousin had enough on his plate without her adding to his worries. She should have guessed Robert's reaction. He regarded compassion as a weakness and passion as a flaw. She should have known, and spared herself the humiliation.

Maya straightened up, zipped her coat up to protect her neck from the wind because she had forgotten her scarf at the office, and started walking toward the restaurant. She would find another way to help Matthew, even if she had to pay for the operation herself. And she could start by granting his wish.

Tristan was yet to arrive when she was escorted to a table by a plump red-haired waitress with smiling eyes. She waited for Maya to sit down, and handed her the menu.

"Here you are, honey. Do you want something to drink?"

"Two San Pellegrino. No ice, one slice of lemon."

The young woman closed her eyes a brief instant before looking up. Arthur sat without waiting for an invitation Maya was not willing to offer anyway.

"Colin told me you were supposed to have lunch here."

Maya made a mental note to talk to Colin about discretion.

"What do you want, Arthur?"

Her tone was biting and he didn't seem to care.

"That boy ..."

"His name is Matthew."

"Yes, Matthew; what is his illness?"

The question surprised her. The waitress brought the drinks and she focused on hers an instant before glancing back to her companion.

"Cancer."

Something flashed in the blue eyes on her, and she momentarily regretted the harsh answer. Abigail, Arthur's mother, had died of cancer too.

"I'm sorry."

He really seemed to be.

"If Moira had accepted me to chair the council, things might not have gone that far."

Once again, his insufferable ego was wiping out all nice thoughts his apparent compassion had brought. Maya put her glass back on the table and folded her arms over her chest.

"I fail to see how you messing with our work would have stopped your father from paralyzing the Foundation's account. I thank God it's just the Foundation he has access to, and not all the hospital money."

"I didn't come here to pick a fight, Maya. I want to offer you a deal."

She glared, threatening. Arthur was no better than his father. A little boy's life was not a thing to *'deal'* with.

"I will convince my father to unfreeze the amount of the surgery despite the financial issue that is currently going on. In return, you will help with this little problem I have."

Arthur asking for a favor didn't sound good. But the money could save Matthew. Maya breathed in slowly and kept hope out of her voice.

"What problem?"

"You pose as my girlfriend for a while."

Her eyes widened in horror. Arthur wanted her to play his new lover so his former girlfriend would stop stalking him? *Please ...*

"This is ridiculous."

"I have my reasons. Think about it, Maya, you can save this little boy's li–" He caught himself quickly. "Matthew's life."

The young man leaned forward toward her, radiating charm and burning blue eyes. She backed instinctively into her chair. Arthur flashed a lazy grin.

"Who knows, you might even discover you like me."

"This has little chance of happening."

From the corner of her eyes, she saw Tristan crossing the street. Maybe Arthur wouldn't remember her cousin; he hadn't seen him in a while. Maya stood.

"I don't think my boyfriend would appreciate it."

Arthur smirked.

"You don't have a boyfriend."

"Who told you such a thing?"

The glance he ran over her casual clothing, worn jeans and simple pullover, gave her a furious impulse to slap him.

"Colin."

Maya made another mental note, this one to kill Colin. Tristan entered the restaurant and the red-haired waitress pointed to their table.

"Well, Colin was mistaken."

She walked swiftly toward her cousin with a brilliant smile, and wrapped her arms around his waist, tiptoeing to murmur in his ear "Please, play along," before she pressed her mouth to his. Tristan returned her embrace for a few seconds before he released her. Arthur stood in turn and approached them, extending one hand.

"Hi, Tristan, nice to see you again. How's Ines?"

Busted. Maya felt the grip on her waist harden. Not only did Arthur remember Tristan, but he knew about his misfortune too. His comment was such a low blow… She wanted to snarl. However, Tristan reacted like the gentleman he was, shaking the offered hand. A certain someone should take lessons.

"Not around anymore, as you can see. Will you share lunch with us?"

"Maybe some other time. Maya, please give me a call later, will you? We need to work out the arrangement for Matthew. Tristan …"

Maya noticed her red scarf was carefully folded on her chair. But when she looked up to thank him, Arthur was already gone.

Chapter 4

Tristan sipped his drink and smiled at Maya who was playing with her fork.

"So the big show was just your ego getting in the way, huh?"

She blushed.

"Sorry about that …"

"I'm not complaining."

Maya smiled at her cousin. Tristan was the real-life image of the romantic poet. Tall and serene, he wore his black hair shoulder-length and looked at the world with dark brown eyes. He was a fine musician and had a knack for mathematics. His easy smile revealed both a nice sense of humor, and an even softer heart, whose only fault had been to fall irrepressibly in love with a woman who had betrayed him, and loved her still.

"Apparently, dear Arthur didn't buy your story."

Arthur and Tristan had never got along well, the contest going way back to childhood when a stronger Arthur used to bully the slight boy her cousin was when he was younger. She sighed.

"I guess not."

"Are you going to accept his offer?"

What she liked most about Tristan was this talent he had to push emotions aside when he needed to analyze things. A talent he failed to apply to Ines, unfortunately.

"Would you?"

"Would I play Arthur's lover to save an eight-year-old boy? As long as he doesn't put his tongue down my throat, anytime."

She laughed and poked at his arm.

"Thanks! Now I'm going to have nightmares about the two of you making out."

Tristan rolled his eyes at the image, grinning. Then his handsome face became serious again.

"Maya, we need to find out what Robert noticed about the finances that made him freeze the Foundation's account."

She opened her mouth to protest but he stopped her.

"I know you still care for your godfather, but you have to accept Robert is only interested in power and money. If he saw a chance to increase his power because something is odd in the books, then there is a good chance he's right. We have to find out what that is."

Maya nodded. Tristan was right. They had to uncover what was wrong with the finances of the Foundation, before Robert found a way to close it for good. They changed the subject for the rest of the meal.

Tristan didn't mention his former girlfriend once, and that was such an improvement—along with the renewed teasing and good humor—that Maya didn't dare ask how he was feeling. They talked about the upcoming holiday, Christmas lists and common friends, future concerts they hoped to attend, or simply enjoyed each other's company in comfortable silence.

*

Tristan stopped his car in front of the hospital.

"Are we still walking the Christmas Market next weekend?"

She smiled happily.

"Definitely!"

"Excellent."

Maya quickly hugged him and hurried toward the building, fighting the biting wind. She avoided going back to the administrative area and walked straight to the playroom the kids used by day hoping to find Matthew there. Reporting her conversation with Robert to Moira could wait; in addition, she had no desire to explain Arthur's bargain. Her sister would probably fret or worse, try to dissuade her from accepting. Not that she had completely made up her mind yet anyway.

The little boy was in a corner sitting on the floor and was playing with a stuffed animal—a horse she guessed, or it could also be a strange-looking camel. Her heart squeezed at the quiet image he made. The other kids welcomed her loudly with enthusiastic greetings and tons of hugs and kisses.

Maya admired each doll and countless toy cars, praised the shaky LEGO constructions and marvelled at several modern art sketches that would have made Picasso jealous. Matthew looked up at the chaos and briefly smiled at her before returning his attention to his toy.

Finally, Maya managed to extract herself from her entourage and went to kneel near him.

"Hello Matthew, are you feeling okay today?"

The little boy vaguely bobbed his head. His lips were a pale pastel color.

"Do you want your oxygen?"

He shook his head. Questions he could answer with a nod or shake were better so he didn't have to speak. Maya caressed the stuffed animal.

"This is a beautiful horse you've got. Do you think I can guess his name?"

Matthew shook his head; his mischievous smile warmed her slightly.

"Let's see. You called him… Flicka."

A shake of the head. Apparently not. Maya frowned as if in concentration.

"Black. Like the horse in the Black Stallion story?"

Another silent '*no*'. The animal was a vivid brown with a flaming mane, after all.

"Hum … You like making things difficult. Is his name Flame?"

Matthew grinned broadly and nodded vigorously.

"It's a beautiful name. You like horses, don't you?"

The little boy was making the animal jump on her knees. He nodded again. Maya moved to lean on the wall beside him.

"We have something special here, it's a Make-a-Wish list. Children make a wish, and if they behave really well, obey the doctors and all, sometimes the wish is granted. Do you want to make a wish too? Of course you'll have to be very very good …"

"Hor…"

The half-mouthed syllable turned into a cough. The young woman waited patiently for the boy to get his breath back, not touching him when all she wanted was to take him in her arms and hug him tight.

After a few excruciating minutes, Matthew plunged brilliant eyes into her own aquamarine ones and gestured at the horse, pushing the animal into her grasp. Maya swallowed, hoping her voice would sound as normal as possible. It broke her heart, to see the little boy fighting for every breath like he did.

"You have a wish about horses?"

Matthew nodded again. She slipped one arm around the frail shoulders gently.

"So this is the deal. You will do your best to get well, and I'll take you to a stud farm. You'll see horses, you'll learn how to tend to them, and we'll go on a long ride together. What do you think?"

The boy sighed quietly, and cuddled against her, eyes closed. Maya kissed his head before enfolding him in her arms completely. If entering Arthur's games meant saving Matthew, it was absolutely worth it. And if she sold her soul to the devil in doing so, then so be it.

*

The door of her apartment thankfully closed behind her, protecting her from the icy wind and the already fallen darkness. It took her less than a minute to take off her coat and light some lamps to create a cheerful glow in the room.

Glancing around, she spotted the box with her Christmas decorations. Maybe she would put some up tonight. Christmas was her favorite time of the year, with all the joy and goodwill sparkling in even the most somber places. Even Moira's very special and horribly out-of-tune interpretation (*execution* was Tristan's definition) of Christmas carols couldn't spoil her fun. She just loved Christmas.

She had yet to buy a Christmas tree. Her friends and family always tried to convince her to buy an artificial one, but she preferred the real thing. Maya didn't care about the inconvenience of buying a new one every year, or the trouble of bringing it to her place. She didn't even mind the constant need to vacuum fallen needles. A real tree was better. It smelled different, it had charm, and especially it was imperfect.

In fact, she made a point every year of finding the ugliest tree she could find and she covered it with all the decorations she had. The poor thing usually turned out to be even more pitiful afterwards, and she totally adored it.

Smiling at the thought, Maya sat to look into the box that contained her Christmas decorations. Most came from her parents. Moira had handed them over gladly, saying that they brought back too many memories, which Maya didn't have because she had been very young when their parents had died. Maya suspected her sister just wanted some excuse to buy new ones, instead of using the kaleidoscopic balls and old tinsel.

The young woman took one tinsel garland out of the box and sighed. The first duty for Christmas decorating was untangling the garlands.

Chapter 5

"Hold on a sec!"

The bell rang again and Maya hurried to the door; the Christmas lights she was trying to untangle clung to her sweater.

Her smile faded under Arthur's stare and crooked eyebrow.

"Do I want to know why you've got glitter all over you?"

"Good evening to you, too. Please close the door; it's cold outside."

Without acknowledging him any further, Maya returned to her previous position in front of the sofa, twisting the free ends of her ornament to untie it. Arthur took off his coat and glanced around with undisguised curiosity.

So this was where she lived. He had expected her to share a flat with Moira, but apparently this was not the case. Save for the Christmas decorations, which had invaded the room, the place was relatively tidy and neat, and small. He would never be able to live with so little space around, especially after growing up at the manor. Maya's apartment was located in a peaceful neighborhood and looked snug, but being inside he felt trapped. Who could bear to stay in a place where only ten steps or so were required to reach the next room?

Arthur looked for a seat. Every flat surface seemed occupied by garlands, some gleaming ornament, or aggressively colored stockings. He picked up one figurine and Maya squealed.

"Be careful!"

Putting down the collectible, he shrugged his shoulders and resigned to stay on his feet.

"You left a message?"

Maya temporarily glanced up.

"Yes; yes I did."

She returned her attention to her work. Arthur repressed a grunt. She was going to make this difficult. He glared at the loose bun on her neck and her thick-framed glasses. Her jeans hinted at long toned legs but her baggy pullover ran well past her hips and hid her body unattractively. This was a bad idea. It was not going to work. He liked his women stylish and ladylike, not covered in torn old clothes and crouched on the floor.

He internally cursed Colin. His friend should have talked him out of it, instead of approving of the ridiculous plan. *'She's not one of your usual bimbos, so people will wonder if it's serious this time. And with Maya, you don't risk her confusing fake feelings with real interest. She knows you.'* Of course, Colin didn't know all of it.

As for knowing him, yes, she knew him well. They had grown up together, after all. As children they had bantered all the time before they definitely fell apart during their teens. They had stopped paying attention to each other then. Arthur was the popular guy, captain of his sports team, dating cheerleaders one after another, and Maya walked the opposite path: science club, charities, et cetera. He tried to remember if she had ever brought a boyfriend home. Probably not; his father would have had a stroke. His reaction now would be something else altogether.

"I'll do it, but I have conditions."

He returned his attention to the floor.

"I'm listening."

Maya finally consented to lever herself to the sofa.

"First, we are not going public until I'm sure Matthew's operation is paid for."

"You will sign a receipt for the check and hand me over guardianship."

She frowned.

"What do you mean *guardianship*?"

"No decision is to be taken about the treatment without my approval."

"But…"

Arthur dismissed her demur.

"P and A is underwriting the loan, so I want to make sure the money is well spent."

Maya gritted her teeth. He was regarding the child as an investment, just like his father would.

"Fine."

The smirk on his face was insufferable.

"Anything else?"

The mocking tone annoyed her, and Maya stood to face him. She was not a petite woman, but he towered over her by a couple of inches. She refused to let the difference in height impress her, and glared.

"How long is this … pretence supposed to last?"

"As long as is necessary. I want my father off my back."

The reply astonished her. She had yet to question his motivations. Arthur's mention of his father hinted there was more to his plot than just scaring some girl away. Maya asked, "What? Why?"

He seemed to relax for a second when he sighed, his shoulders moving down a little; then he stiffened again.

"Arranged marriage is not in my upcoming plans."

She grinned and a small laugh escaped her.

"You have to admit, Arthur, your father trying to marry you off is funny."

"I fail to see how this is amusing."

The flat tone sobered her at once.

"Obviously."

Maya stepped back, arms crossed over her chest.

"Kissing stays chaste. No unnecessary flirting or touching."

The young man sneered.

"Should I return the compliment?"

She made a face at him.

"You think you're that irresistible? Let me tell y…"

The unexpected kiss created a throb inside her, her heart suddenly beating faster. Her hands came up to rest on his chest. Maybe Arthur saw an invitation in the gesture, for the pressure on her mouth became more insistent and her skin warmed instantly. She used her hold on him as leverage to shove him off.

"What do you think you're doing?"

The pang of desire that shot through him when he touched her mouth threw Arthur off balance. He didn't understand why her lips were moving on their own accord instead of parting under his for a deeper kiss. *'What do you think you're doing?'*

Suddenly, he realized she had pushed him away. Women didn't do that, not to him. Maya could not be different. She too must have felt the heat building between them.

Very annoyed with his own reaction, Arthur stood his ground when all he wanted was to lean forward again. He smirked.

"I needed to make sure you're up for the role, of course."

Her face remained expressionless. Only the sharp intake of air and a brief gleam in her eyes told him he had hit a nerve. Her stare fixed on him was as cold as ice. Arthur's mocking smile grew into a downright leer.

The staring contest lasted for another moment before she spoke again.

"You will treat me with respect and politeness, like a real person, and not like some disposable doll. And this applies to every situation, public *AND* private."

Arthur frowned.

"I treat women decently."

"You'll have to prove that."

"Are you done?"

Her *suitor* went on before she could even nod.

"Our arrangement must stay a secret. I suppose you told Tristan; Colin knows about it too, and that's it. If your sister or other friends ask about it, tell them I helped convince my father for the boy's sake, and it pleased you."

"It would mean I liked you before."

"Didn't you?"

The conceited tone was really too much to take.

"Aargh! Do you have to sound so superior all the time?!"

The outburst surprised him and reminded him of her harangue to his father in the morning, of older ardent battles, of the heat raised by a vague brush of lips… He would have to remember how passionate she could be, if he didn't want the whole scheme to blow up in his face. Arthur held up his hands in a mute apology.

Maya sighed, already calm once more. Then she frowned again, though this time it was more worry than anger that shadowed her face.

"Your father won't be pleased. Not only are you challenging him by refusing his candidate but you are courting *me*."

"I'll take the risk."

His answer surprised her even more. Arthur seemed unconcerned about upsetting his father. Robert used to interview her boyfriends like a Spanish inquisitor whenever she dared bring them to the manor, and now he apparently couldn't stand her any more. There was more to this than met the eye. It should make her suspicious. Yet God help her, she was curious.

"Okay then… What's next?"

"Next? Colin is taking a look at your wardrobe."

Chapter 6

Maya tried to push up her glasses, only to realize once more she wasn't wearing any. The lack of weight on her nose was still bothering her, but at least she had gotten over the '*I-feel-naked*' phase. And she had to admit, the surprised (and sometimes appreciative) looks of her coworkers were worth the ten minutes it had taken her to put the contact lenses in this morning.

She caught her reflection in the window. Contact lenses were not the only change Colin had suggested (*imposed* had been more like it). He and Gavin had spent one complete evening inspecting her closet only to reach the conclusion that Maya was in desperate need of a shopping trip, with Arthur's credit card.

The fact that the owner of the card had not even argued about it had annoyed her beyond reason. Her clothes were perfect for her work and the other activities she had! She was perfectly capable of paying for her own clothing, thank you very much. Making a *'pretty woman'* out of her was absolutely out of the question, and not part of the bargain. She was not Arthur's customary snobbish fashion starlet and it was exactly for that reason that Arthur was supposed to have fallen for *her*.

After a two-hour battle, Colin had finally convinced her to buy a couple of pieces, to complement her own wardrobe. So today she was wearing her favorite jeans, which fortunately had escaped the cut, with a fitted red blouse and matching lipstick. She liked the blouse. The fabric was smooth, and the color was cheerfully bright. As for the lipstick …

The light knock on the door brought her back from her reverie.

"Miss Finnegan? You have a visitor."

"Thanks. Oh ... Hello, Arthur."

Hopefully, to her curious assistant, her blush could pass for the simple pleasure of seeing Arthur rather than the shame of having been caught off guard when he stepped in her office. At a loss of what to do, she was glad he took the initiative, even if the hug and quick peck on her cheek felt awkward.

Arthur released her as soon as he heard the door close behind them. He kept his voice low nonetheless.

"You have to learn to relax when I touch you or no one is going to believe us."

It vexed her to feel her cheeks growing even warmer at the patronizing tone. Maya forced a smile on her face before she asked, "Did you come for Matthew?"

He caught the hint instantly. *'We are not going public before the payment is secured.'*

"Yes, indeed. I have all the papers here."

To an outsider, the exchange could have appeared quite innocent, Maya thought. Still there was a less than subtle warning behind his engaging smile and gentle words. She had to remember he was not a friend. Arthur had his own agenda in their little masquerade, and the help he was offering was not unconditional.

Arthur placed a thin file in front of her. Maya slowly opened it. It contained only one envelope and two sheets of paper, all embossed with the Pendletons & Associates coat of arms. She paused when she recognized the logo.

"I thought Robert had changed the dragon?"

"He did. I just like this one better."

The chimera was delicately detailed, with subtle shades of dark gold to enhance the impression of movement. Abigail had been a fantastic artist. She liked this one better too, compared to the modern stylish beast Robert had chosen to replace it with. She wanted to say so to her visitor, but Arthur had turned to walk to the window.

Maya began reading the papers carefully. The first one was explaining that Arthur, on behalf of P&A, was accepting legal responsibility for the child for as long as treatments were required. Her signature, as a representative of the Foundation's board, was necessary to submit all medical decisions to his approval beforehand. She picked up her pen, and inscribed her name next to his.

The second paper was a receipt. Maya gasped.

"Arthur, this is way too much! The operation will cost half that…"

"I wish to avoid going to my father a second time about this."

Maya swallowed the coming unkind answer and opened the envelope.

Arthur approved internally. Most people considered paperwork a dull and annoying task to get rid of as soon as possible. Maya, however, was caring enough to make sure Matthew would be properly taken care of, and that no bias had escaped her. Her attention to that little detail suited him.

The amount on the bank note was the same one as on the receipt. Maya signed the receipt too, and handed back the papers to Arthur who put them in his briefcase.

"I'll send you a copy."

"Thank you."

Her gratitude referred to more than the paperwork. He bowed his head courteously. Uneasy, Maya looked for something to say next.

A noise in the corridor cut through the growing silence. Arthur moved to the door and offered his arm with a cheeky smile.

"I've yet to meet my charge. Shall we?"

While they went to the south wing where Matthew shared a room with another child, Maya grew animated quickly, describing the layout of the hospital and how it created an optimal environment for the ill children. She was working with the logistics department, and Moira was in human resources.

He knew that of course. He had studied the charts and organization plans. Arthur bore her babbling more or less patiently. Having her behaving normally was better than her frightened mouse jitters.

Several nurses started whispering behind their backs while they progressed along the busy corridors. The envious looks came from both men and women. The former intrigued him, and Arthur glimpsed at her while exiting the elevator.

She looked nicer today. The crimson color flattered her ivory skin and ebony hair. For once, he could really see her face. Maya had interesting features: full lips, delicately curved, and a straight nose. Her high cheekbones gave her a feline air. She had cat's eyes too—almond-shaped and of a very pale green.

His examination put her ill at ease again and she walked away from him to knock lightly on a door.

Two children were settled in bed, one reading a comic book and the other playing with a toy car. Both smiled happily when Maya entered. She waved back with a brilliant smile. Once properly kissed and hugged, the boys stared at Arthur.

"Is he your boyfriend?" asked the one with the car.

Arthur beat her to the answer, approaching the beds in turn to shake hands with the curious boys. He glanced briefly at the embarrassed woman before he smiled.

"I'm working on that. I'm Arthur."

"My name is Mark. Him, it's Matthew. He doesn't speak much; it hurts."

Arthur knew that too. The simple truth stung nonetheless. The silent boy had wrapped his tiny arms around Maya so his black-haired head rested on her stomach. An oxygen mask hanged from a pole near the bed.

Arthur looked away. Mark's chatty mood chased away the growing discomfort.

"Doctor said I can go home in two weeks. I'll be home for Christmas! I miss my dog … but not my little sister. She's such a baby."

"You were quite happy to see her last weekend," Maya interjected.

"I suppose."

Arthur winked.

"I grew up with two girls. They can be a pain."

The tease earned him a glare from Maya, who had sat on the bed near her protégé to read the comic with him.

His big announcement made, Mark gestured for Arthur to pick up a car in the display on his bedside table.

"You can have the police one if you want. I like the yellow. Let's play 'Cops and Robbers'!"

Arthur grinned, and took off his jacket.

"You won't win at this one."

They started a fierce chase all over the hospital bed. Mark's shrill laugh echoed in the room when Arthur lost his grip on the small car while running it on the metallic rail. Maya looked up. He was fumbling with the sheets to find his toy, and his smile was the first genuine one she had seen on him in years.

All smiles disappeared when the door banged open.

"What is he doing here?"

Chapter 7

Moira's angry voice glaringly contrasted with Mark's victorious yells. Maya gently pushed Matthew away and came to face her sister, while Arthur arranged his tie, all relaxed expression gone.

"Arthur is …"

"He's Maya's boyfriend!"

Moira's eyes narrowed dangerously. Maya glanced down under their intense scrutiny. Arthur stepped between the two sisters and shook the hand that was ready to grab Maya's wrist; to the kids, it could look like the salute had been intended all along.

"Good morning, Moira."

She pulled away abruptly. Maya noticed a slight tremor in her hands and she dreaded the upcoming storm.

"Arthur is handling Matthew's medical help, Moira. We're just …"

"We are *rediscovering* each other."

The tranquil affirmation dragged Moira's attention back to him. Her lips were so severely pinched they formed a very thin line of hatred. However, she kept her composure. Maya used the temporary truce to quickly kiss the children before she slipped her arm under her sister's to walk out of the room. Arthur winked at the boys and followed.

The atmosphere in Maya's office was glacial. As soon as the door closed behind them, Moira exploded.

"You can't date him! He's a Pendleton! That's nonsense! You hate guys like him!"

The avalanche of reproaches didn't even connect with each other. Arthur smirked.

"Can you define *'guys like me'*?"

The cheeky comment caused more murderous glances from the enraged woman.

"Define you? Conceited, arrogant, blunt, a womanizer, obnoxious, a snob, cold-blooded ..."

The list went on. The more Moira added unflattering epithets, the more Arthur stiffened despite the mocking smile plastered on his face.

Maya feared he would lose his patience and say something irreparable. She interrupted the furious monologue.

"Please, Moira... Everybody deserves a second chance. Arthur is not Robert. His help with Matthew means a lot to me. And I want to get to know him better."

Her intercession didn't work.

"You can't trust him! Don't be ridiculous, he's going to break your heart and..."

"I'm sorry you don't approve but I'm a big girl and I'm free to see whomever I want."

Maya's convinced tone unsettled him. Each word sounded truthful. Arthur smiled back at her (a real smile this time) without really thinking. Her sister snorted but swallowed her wrath and exited the room, looking daggers at Arthur from over her shoulder.

Maya immediately stepped away from him.

"She's very angry. Did you notice her eyes?"

"Yes, I noticed."

He collected his things.

"I've got to go. I'll call you later about tomorrow's dinner."

"What dinner?"

Arthur grinned; his smile held a touch of good humor under the tease.

"I faced your dragon. Now it's your turn."

*

The coffee in his mug was barely warm. Arthur put it back on his desk without drinking.

He had spent more time at the hospital than he had originally intended and he had been running behind ever since. Besides the Foundation's case, which his father had consented to entrust to him, several other projects reclaimed his attention.

Arthur scratched his head and then rolled his shoulders, trying to ease the tension building in his neck. People thought he had an easy life, enjoying himself because his father was one of the most powerful men in the country. The truth was that collecting drinks and women was just a way to ease the pressure. God knew he needed the release after working twelve hours a day, six days a week to live up to his father's standards of excellence.

'Mr. Pendleton? Your father on line two.'

"Thanks, Lucy."

Arthur pressed one key and his father's strong voice filled the room.

'Where do you stand with the Foundation?'

No greetings, no polite introduction from Robert Pendleton.

"I—"

His father interrupted before he could even start a full sentence.

'I want the fraud exposed ASAP, Arthur. This little commerce can't go on. You asked to be in charge of the case,

I'm expecting that you close it, and fast. What about the Mercia contract?'

"Nearly done. You'll want to review some items about quotas and income taxes. It'll be completed tom "

Robert cut in again. Arthur felt a pulsing on his temples, announcing the headache.

'I need that tonight.'

Tonight. It was five already. Arthur shook his head to clear it of the louder pounding.

"Yes, Father."

'Regis and his daughter arrive tomorrow morning. I count on you to escort Isobel to the welcoming cocktail party.'

There they were.

"I already have a date for the event, Father."

The silence on the other end of the line was heavy. And it lasted longer than was comfortable. Arthur swallowed. Long silences from his father were rarely a good thing.

'I see.'

Sharp words. Icy tone. He was glad Robert had flown on the other side of the country unexpectedly to close off that deal.

'Have that contract and the tender documents sent by eight tomorrow morning.'

The characteristic sound of a rough hang-up reverberated in his head, already heavy with the newborn migraine.

No good-bye, either. Arthur searched his drawer for aspirin. Finishing both the contract and the TD for the Mercia deal by 8 a.m. meant working around the clock, again.

Colin was supposed to have dinner with Gavin's parents, yet he would cancel if asked. Arthur gulped two pills with the rest of his coffee. He would achieve more work if he flew solo.

*

Of course he hadn't called. She had expected him to, for some time, before she tired of postponing her evening projects in case the phone rang.

Maya signalled to the driver she was getting off. If Arthur thought she was going to bend to his every command and make herself available for last minute plans, he was sorely mistaken.

She stepped off the bus and crossed the street carefully, keeping her eyes down to avoid stepping into the melted snow.

"Hi."

Maya glanced up, startled. His face held the marks of a restless night, no doubt partying until dawn. He wore a different shirt and tie, so apparently he had gone home to shower and change; yet she wondered if he had slept at all.

At least his breath when he lightly kissed her cheek didn't smell of alcohol. His hold on her was a little rough. It reminded her of a child seeking comfort. More likely the exhaustion was wearing out his control.

Maya mastered her instincts that were yelling at her to step back as quickly as possible.

"Can I offer breakfast to make up for not calling?"

The suggestion amazed her. He almost sounded sincere. Almost.

"You should go to bed. You look terrible."

The young man took her arm to escort her toward the building, whether vaguely amused or annoyed, she couldn't tell.

"You think I was out clubbing all night long, don't you. Sorry to disappoint, Edana. My father needed some documents early this morning."

Robert had nicknamed her Edana, 'little fire' in Irish. Maya chased away the bittersweet memory, and returned her attention back to Arthur who was holding the door. It was just past eight. How late had he worked? She felt a little bad to have automatically presumed the worst of him.

"The cocktail party is at the Grand Hotel. Hopefully Father won't make a scene with a crowd around. It starts at six-thirty but …"

"Slow down a minute, will you? What cocktail party?"

Impatience flared in the blue eyes and dismissed all ideas of offering coffee.

"We are attending the annual cocktail party Pendletons & Associates holds for its major clients tonight. First, the cocktail party and next week, the Ball. You can't have forgotten that much about us."

"But …"

"I'm tired Maya, and I'm not in the mood for a fruitless argument. I'll pick you up at seven."

Arthur brushed her cheek again, and left her gawping in the hall. Maya composed herself quickly, hoping no one had noticed the scene. She wanted to stomp her foot. Why hadn't he told her the previous day? How was she supposed to be ready by seven? This arrangement was impossible. *HE* was impossible!

Chapter 8

Maya fumbled with her clothes once again. She had already searched her closet three times trying to find an appropriate outfit, to no avail. In desperate need of advice, she had called Colin twice, getting his voicemail both times. Moira, who often shared her own extensive wardrobe with her, had flat-out refused to help. '*I don't want to hear about your mess with the Pendletons.*'

Tristan knocked and entered with two mugs. Maya took hers gratefully, and wrapped her fingers around the hot cup.

"Help me! I don't know what to do. I obviously can't wear pants and the only dress I have is just plain."

"You're nervous."

The tea threatened to spill when she jerked, readying herself to contest his statement. She was not nervous! She was… Fine, nervous. A little. A lot. Horribly. Oh boy …

Tristan examined her flaming face an instant before he spoke again.

"You should cancel. This whole arrangement is not a good idea."

"I thought you came to help?"

Maya burned her tongue sipping her tea and put it away to cool. Her dress lay on the bed and she held it in front of her, looking at the effect in the mirror. Tristan tried again.

"I understand you gave your word, but I don't want to see you hurt."

"Robert can't do or say any worse than he already has."

"I'm not worried about Robert."

Tristan being Tristan, he could not make it clearer to whom he was referring. His comment brought up a smile, chasing away the nerves.

"Arthur won't do anything improper. He promised to behave. You know him; he considers honoring his word to be sacred, as if he were chairing the Round Table or something."

"If you say so."

"He offered twice the amount Matthew needed, you know."

Her cousin didn't insist. Maya had apparently resolved to overlook Arthur's faults for the time being and keep her part of their strange bargain. He could only hope their little plot would not turn her world upside-down. Maya's heart was too soft not to fall into the trap if Arthur decided to add some side benefits to his original plan. Which he was perfectly capable of.

Tristan chose to change the subject.

"With a scarf and your mother's pearls, you'll look fantastic."

Maya beamed, then her smile faded.

"Oh no. Moira borrowed the pearls. She was supposed to hand them back, but we both forgot."

"You'll be lovely anyway. You always are."

He paused an instant before asking, smiling back at the delightful grin the compliment had brought forth:

"What time is Arthur coming for you?"

"He said seven … Oh Lord, it's already six-thirty. Out!"

Maya pushed her cousin out of the room and hurried toward the bathroom.

*

SECOND CHANCES

When Maya entered the living room a little after seven, Tristan and Arthur were engaged in a glacial exchange of banalities. She could hardly tell which one of the two contestants was the most relieved to see her.

Tristan moved first, offering his arm. She appreciated the gesture. Arthur was looking at her with an unreadable frown.

She looked … intriguing. She had chosen a simple black dress with a discreet square neck. The white scarf fitted on her bare shoulders enhanced the fact she wore no jewels, except the small pearls at her ears. The lack of jewels didn't bother him. In fact, the way her understated looks appealed to him was unexpected *and* uncomfortable.

Arthur realized he was staring and glanced away, playing with the keys in his hand while Tristan helped her with her coat.

"I'll stay if you want."

The offer had Arthur reacting instantly.

"I don't know what time I'll bring Maya home."

"I don't mind waiting."

Tension grew between the two men again, this time their jesting growing less civil by the minute. Maya squeezed her cousin's arm gently.

"I'll be fine, Tristan. It's just a cocktail. What can go wrong?"

*

A lot could.

First, she had felt totally overwhelmed by the loud crowd after the flashes from the official photographer had blinded her. Afterwards, Robert had turned bright red when he had caught sight of the two of them. Then, Arthur had disappeared—God only knew where—just minutes after their arrival; not that she missed his company, anyway. And then, Maya suddenly realized she wouldn't be able to eat anything from the buffet because everything seemed to contain seafood, to which she was allergic. And of course that stupid scarf kept sliding, so she had to stay with her elbows glued to her sides to keep it in place.

"Maya!"

Colin's voice seemed like the most delightful sound she had ever heard. Her friend was holding two plates and offered one, but Maya shook her head.

"I can't ... Seafood."

The young man jumped back, pulling the plates as far from her as possible, and she chuckled.

"Don't worry, I am not going to suffer anaphylactic shock just because I smell shrimp."

He blushed and put one plate away to attack his smoked salmon blinis.

"Where is Arthur?"

"Some matters required my son's immediate attention."

The freezing voice of Robert startled her and Maya tightened her grip on her scarf instinctively before she turned around.

The matters in question were a bald man and a pretty blonde in a pink dress, on the other side of the room. Given Arthur's stiff demeanour, she supposed he was paying his respects to the intended blushing bride.

Maya tried a quiet a smile, though she was sure it looked more like a pout.

"Good evening, Robert."

She went completely rigid when he embraced her. The murmur in her ear was nothing like his apparent welcome.

"Your dirty operations are a shame to your father's name. Enjoy your power while it lasts as we *will* wipe out your business, whatever the cost. Arthur will come back to his senses soon enough. You won't be able to bewitch him so he forgets his duty. Besides, he tends to tire of pretty things rather easily."

Maya pushed away from her godfather as discreetly as she could.

"But *you* don't tire, do you Robert? Why do you hate me so much? I am your ward, you are supposed to lov…"

'Love me'. 'Protect me'. 'Support me'. 'Be happy when I am'. She stopped mid-sentence, and turned her head away without waiting for an answer; tears of anger and hurt glimmered in her eyes. Arthur, who had apparently decided his *date* was worth his attention after all and reappeared by her side, wrapped one arm around her. Maya had to make an effort not to slap his hand away.

She wished he'd said something, presented apologies for his father or his own desertion but his face was blank. Maya tried to compose herself so she could smile at him like the loving girlfriend she was supposed to be, but failed.

Robert just shrugged his shoulders and left without a word.

Colin, who was in fact responsible for Arthur's sudden reappearance, reacted first to save the situation.

"Maya, you're awfully pale. Tell me you didn't try the mousse. There's shellfish in that, your allergies!"

He elbowed Arthur hard in the chest; the young man was finally shaken out of his immobility.

"Are you okay? Do you need your anti-histamine drug?"

Playing along with their scheme was easier than pretending she was all right.

"I didn't eat anything but I don't feel that great... I'd like to sit a moment…"

"Of course."

Maybe the charade held some truth. She *was* feeling light-headed. Maya had to lean against Arthur for balance and she hated needing him. The grasp on her waist as he helped her up the stairs to a quieter area was hard and she wanted to qualify it as unpleasant. She rejected the idea his warmth was comforting. The fussing was just a fake and it'd better stay that way.

*

While Colin went down to the kitchens to ask for something she would be able to eat, Arthur settled her on a couch in the nearly empty rotunda of the hotel, and sat near her, turning so he could face her.

He could guess well enough what his father had murmured in her ear. *'We will see that your masquerade of a charity is reduced to dust. Arthur is just playing with you. You will regret the day you refused to listen to me.'*

He'd had his share of the lecture, hissed in an empty room only minutes after they arrived.

'Is that how you intend to find your way to their dirty operations?'

'I thought you had learned by now not to mix business with pleasure.'

'The Finnegan sisters are nothing but liars and cheats.'

'Enjoy her bed, she is attractive after all, but keep clear of her poisonous ways.'

All remarks were equally insulting. Arthur wondered why it was taking Colin so long to obtain some chopped vegetables and fruit.

Maya had briefly glanced at the falling snow through the impressive bay window, before returning her attention to him. Arthur chose to break the silence before her stare disturbed him further. His traitorous mind came back to the more personal comments about Maya and he dismissed them quickly. Only the fact that Robert had swallowed the bait was important.

"My father bought it."

She frowned at the self-satisfied tone in his voice.

"Apparently so. Can you explain why Pendletons & Associates is so keen on destroying our Foundation?"

SECOND CHANCES

Chapter 9

"Can you explain why Pendletons & Associates is so keen on destroying our Foundation?"

The question drifted in the air, soft-spoken despite the harsh reality it disclosed. The edge in the piercing green eyes fixed on him told Arthur hurt had given way to anger. He was familiar with the feeling. The idea of being associated with his father's crusade was equally troubling.

"This is not the place to discuss that."

Maya narrowed her eyes. This was the typical Pendleton reaction. *'Don't lie but avoid giving straight answers whenever you can.'*

"Then I suggest you bring me home. Maybe Tristan will still be there, I'm sure he is going to be very interested in what you have to say, too."

"We can't leave now."

"Why not?"

A waiter approached them, and Arthur's impenetrable expression changed into a more open one, charming and playful.

"I think we need a drink. Two Kir Royales, please."

The waiter nodded and left.

Her annoyance was growing by the minute; he could feel it in the tension in her shoulders. Unfortunately, he had to rely on her self-control to keep up the pretence.

"It would be too much out of character for me to leave this early."

Me. Me. Me. The guy was redefining narcissism! Maya closed her eyes in order to ignore the urge to hit him. She couldn't shout at him either, but she could always bite.

"A considerate man would bring his girlfriend home, if she's not feeling well."

The comment was more effective than a slap. Arthur straightened his back, and took his arm off the backseat behind her, ready to stand.

"You're right. Please give me five minutes to …"

Suddenly she restrained him, curling her fingers around his arm with a shy smile. Arthur froze, completely stunned by her volte-face, until he saw the waiter coming back with their drinks. He relaxed just long enough for the man to smile at the couple holding hands in the loveseat.

The golden pink liquid in her glass was fizzing. Curiosity won over anger.

"What's that?"

The topic of cocktails was a safer one. Arthur answered eagerly.

"Kir Royale is champagne with crème de cassis, a blackcurrant liqueur."

Maya sipped it tentatively and smiled, a real smile this time.

"I like it."

Arthur drained half of his own. The gesture brought a shadow to her face but Maya said nothing. He took the hint anyway.

"I need more than one glass to get drunk, Maya."

She looked away. Conversation eluded her. She knew nothing of his tastes in music, movies or books; the things she knew about him, his party ways, his work, his relationship with his father, were off limits. There was only one thing they had shared so far …

"Matthew needs to have some tests done: blood check, scans, general check-up, and then the operation will be scheduled."

"Do you think it will be long before he can be operated on? He seems … frail."

Pain flashed in her eyes, and Arthur momentarily regretted asking. Her attention lingered on the candle on the table in front of her before she took another sip of her cocktail.

"You're good with kids."

"You sound surprised."

Maya sighed. Even in a quiet conversation Arthur could not help automatically defending himself for being human. It made her temper flare once more.

"Of course I am. It's unlike you to notice smaller ones."

This time, he chose to speak up against the accusation.

"I like kids. They understand a lot more than most adults think. And they know that winning a toy car race is really an important thing."

Her smile was a little dreamy, probably at the remembrance of Mark's enthusiasm. He had to be careful. It was not like him to talk about himself. Maybe the alcohol was wiping off what fatigue had not yet shattered.

Thinking about the children at the hospital brought back other subjects, which Arthur had no desire to discuss just now. Did she know her sister was a junkie? Did she know her soon to be brother-in-law was her supplier? By now, he was sure Maya didn't share Moira's addiction. She looked so innocent. How innocent was she?

Arthur finished his drink and glanced around. They were alone in the rotunda now. Colin was nowhere to be seen. How could it take that long to get some chopped vegetables and fruit?

He asked, in spite of his own good sense,

"How far would you go for those kids?"

'How far would you go? You accepted to 'date' me for some money to save one orphan. Would you accept or help with drug trafficking? How far would you really go?' The question brought her attention back to him.

"Not that far."

The answer and her glare puzzled him, until he realized his fingers were still linked with hers, possessively settled just above her knee. Arthur took off his hand immediately.

"That was not what I meant."

"What did you mean, then?"

And then they were back at the beginning. Arthur gestured for another drink. Sighing, Maya looked around the room once more. She wished Colin would come back soon.

*

It was late when Arthur drove her back to her apartment. She wanted to get rid of him as soon as possible, but unfortunately he accompanied her to the door, waiting while she fumbled with her key to unlock it.

The wind had risen once more, and her outfit was not exactly made for winter's icy gusts of air. Goosebumps were torturing her. Her fingers were numb from the cold.

"Please. Let me."

He took the key from her reluctant hand and unlocked the door quickly.

"Here."

"Thank you. I'd like to say I had fun, but I'm not that good at lying."

Her provocative honesty amused him. The grin seemed nearly genuine.

"You'll improve with time. Next Saturday."

"I'm busy on Saturday."

He frowned. Maya stepped into her apartment and Arthur followed.

"Tristan and I are walking the Christmas Market, and we'll probably rent a movie afterward."

"Are you and Tristan romantically involved?"

Maya laughed; his displeasure grew. The question was legitimate. She had presented her cousin as her lover, that first day… Of course, he had dismissed the idea but…

"Tristan and I? God, no…"

She paused, her nose wrinkling in curiosity.

"Why are you asking?"

Uncomfortable with the satisfaction her denial had given him, Arthur retreated behind his trademark smirk.

"We are dating and you intend to spend one whole day with another man; I have to ask."

"We're not–"

He interrupted her again. One of these days, she was going to tell him exactly how annoying this habit was.

"For the public eyes, we are. I'll come with you."

Her eyes widened. Arthur intended to join them for shopping and their monthly video-fest? With Tristan, who couldn't stand him? So her cousin would be forced to watch their pseudo-flirting? Was he mad? Trying to drive her crazy?

"I don't think this is a good idea."

"Do you prefer to cancel your plans?"

"I'm not going to cancel!"

"Then I'll be there."

He surprised her again by brushing a kiss on her cheek. They were alone, there was no need to display some inexistent affection.

"I'll come by tomorrow morning to sign the check-up papers for Matthew. Sweet dreams."

Chapter 10

Maya glanced at her watch. The first tests were scheduled in twenty minutes, and without Arthur's signature, she would have to postpone them. He had promised to come by to sign the papers but he had yet to show up. This was just like the phone call. Arthur was absolutely unreliable when it came to …

"Miss Finnegan? Visitors."

Finally!

She spun on her heels, showing her best all-teeth smile when all she wanted was to rip his throat open.

The first person to enter the room was not Arthur, however. The blonde she had spotted the previous evening stepped in, smiling widely. Maya frowned. What was *she* doing here?

"Hello, Maya, isn't it? I'm Isobel."

Before she could shake the offered hand, one strong arm circled her waist and Arthur's mouth crashed on hers. Maya felt heat spreading through her as soon as he touched her lips.

The kiss ended almost as abruptly as it began, but he kept her close for another second, just long enough for Maya to feel his heartbeat through his shirt, matching her hurried one. She should not react like that to his touch. They were just playing a role, nothing more.

And they had not officially graduated to the *kissing-on-the-mouth* stage yet. At least she thought they hadn't.

The sheepish smile he flashed was another first.

"Sorry to be late, Edana. Father suggested I show Isobel the city while he discusses business with Regis. She loves children and given that I was coming here…"

"Oh."

The small word was all she could muster before her surprising embarrassment gave way to amusement. So Arthur had been framed by his father again.

Her 'suitor' misunderstood her silence.

"You don't mind giving her a tour, do you? I'll stay with Matthew during the check-up."

The name finally cleared her head from the ghost of his embrace.

"The papers on my desk, you need to ..."

Arthur moved to the table and sat there to read, grabbing a pen as if he was at his own desk. If he started chewing on it, she was going to kill him.

Maya faced the blonde woman in front of her. Isobel was her exact opposite: blonde, pretty, sophisticated, and perfectly at ease with the odd situation.

"I think your work is fantastic. I wish my father would let me do something like that. Arthur told me everything about it. He can't stop babbling about you anyway and he was only too happy to satisfy my curiosity."

The blonde winked. Maya turned to her 'boyfriend' who was still conscientiously scanning the documents before signing them. She was sure Arthur was anything but the babbling type. However, his ears seemed a little red. She smiled back at Isobel.

"Arthur probably embellished it all. My work is not that exciting. I'm just one step above the housekeeper."

The other woman refused the modesty.

"Don't underestimate your work. One is always grateful for decent meals and fresh clothes. Sometimes, it's the only thing that saves the day."

The papers made their way back onto her desk.

"Done. Isobel, can you excuse us for a minute?"

"Of course. I'll wait outside."

She danced out of the room with a complicit grin, which made Maya blush from head to toe. Arthur sighed as soon as they were alone, his shoulders visibly relaxing. Maya grinned.

"She seems nice. Are you sure you don't want to reconsider?"

He stiffened.

"She's not my type."

"Hmm … Cute, blonde, sparkly, well-bred; she looks a lot like your type."

"Are you trying to annoy me?"

Her laugher erupted in the silent room. It felt good to have some leverage, to initiate the tease for once. His eyes had turned a darker blue as he was leaning against her desk, ankles crossed and arms folded over his chest. A great pose for *GQ* or *Forbes* magazine.

She grinned but took another step back before his proximity disturbed her further.

"Yes, and I got you. Now stop pouting or your future bride may question our 'private' interlude."

"Wait."

Her hand was already on the doorknob and she glanced over her shoulder at the call. Her braided hair was falling in complicated twists near the small of her back. Her gray wool dress flattered her figure, nicely clinging to her curves. Arthur shook the thought away.

"I need to know. Did you talk to Moira? About the Foundation?"

"My discussions with my sister about the Foundation are none of your business."

Arthur tried to bury the twist of anger her answer stirred inside him.

Maya ignored the glare.

"Thanks to your little game, she refuses to discuss anything related to P and A and she's–"

She trailed off and turned toward the door again, chin pointing up proudly. Her voice held traces of hurt, behind the blatant annoyance. His hand settled on her shoulder. The gesture surprised them both; Maya escaped his touch by stealth.

"I'll give Isobel a very quick tour, so I can come back for Matthew shortly."

The change of subject suited him.

"Not too quick, please. I'm stuck with her until we met Regis and my father for lunch."

"Poor little baby."

Arthur scowled before he plastered a grin on his face and opened the door.

*

The way toward the south wing had never seemed so long to Maya. Isobel was chatting happily, teasing Arthur about some personal habits Maya didn't know about and would have overlooked gladly. Of course, their 'pairing' made it impossible to show it.

"You seem to know each other well."

The slight rasp in her voice was not jealousy. Absolutely not. Isobel laughed.

"We've met a few times. Arthur has never tried to seduce me and I have never stopped harassing him. All things considered, we get along pretty well. That's probably why our fathers came up with that stupid plan of theirs."

Maya ogled at her new acquaintance.

"You know?"

"Of course I do! Robert is as subtle as a brick and my father is not much better. Even after seeing Arthur with you yesterday, they gave it another try this morning. 'Spend the day together, have fun, you must have a lot to talk about,' and blah blah blah … But you have nothing to worry about. Arthur is obviously totally smitten with you and I need someone who can take pieces of advice here and there without considering his manhood is being injured."

"Good luck with that." Arthur grunted, uncertain of which part had bothered him the most: the 'totally smitten' absurdity or the fact that Isobel had accused him of machismo. He also didn't like the amused spark in Maya's eyes. The hilarity, however, flew away when his hand settled on the small of her back, as he escorted her inside the elevator.

Of course it was pride that drove him to do so, only pride. As they started moving up, Arthur kept his arm around her just for the satisfaction of feeling her discomfort.

The constant questioning about the Foundation and its management were more than enough to distract her without the need to add Arthur's hand brushing on her back. Maya moved slightly to shake it off.

"By the way, what were the papers Arthur had to handle back in your office?"

Arthur gulped some inexistent saliva, momentarily taken aback. He should have remembered that Isobel was not just a pretty face, but her father's daughter, observant and cunning. Maya turned to the blonde, gracefully pushing her braid off her shoulder. The movement recaptured his attention momentarily.

"Arthur is one of our little patients' guardian angel. The Foundation can't rely only on the revenue from our financial investments, even if we are doing pretty well. Donations are always welcomed, especially at this time of the year.

Pendletons and Associates have been particularly generous this year," Maya explained.

He swallowed again. Her hand was now locked around his elbow, and Maya was looking at him with big shiny eyes.

His 'girlfriend' had spoken nothing but the truth; still, she had twisted it a little so suspicion was diverted and then added some comedy for good measure. She even sounded admiring. Arthur made a mental note to remember she could act quite well.

Isobel grinned.

"I'd say Arthur had ulterior motives when he suggested the Foundation be awarded a P and A donation."

Maya tightened her grip on his arm. *He* suggested the Foundation be awarded a donation? Not likely. '*Just a façade, Maya... Keep it up.*'

"I really don't know what makes you say that."

The blonde woman just giggled and Maya sighed internally.

The eight-year-old boy was alone; his roommate was in the playroom. Matthew glanced up immediately when they entered and smiled at Maya. She walked briskly to his bed and sat there, taking him into her arms.

"Hi. You're going to see some doctors this morning."

The boy stiffened and hugged his horse tightly. Maya caressed his head gently.

"There's nothing to be afraid of. I'll join you very soon, but I have some things to do first. Arthur will be with you in the meantime. You remember him? He is my friend."

Matthew nodded silently, his clear eyes moving to Arthur while he cuddled against the young woman. Maya kissed his hair and rested her cheek on his head.

"You'll be good, and we'll talk more about your wish this afternoon, okay?"

The lovely picture brought a gentle smile to Isobel's features. She peeked at Arthur, who was stoically looking at them.

"Who is the boy?"

"Matthew is an orphan."

"Maya seems to care about him a great deal."

"Yes, she does."

She paused and asked, "What is so special about her, Arthur? You're generally not so cautious around women."

He turned his full attention back to the blonde, with the sickening feeling that she was seeing right through him. Arthur arched an eyebrow in a silent dare but Isobel refused to recoil.

"You'd better know what you're doing. She's completely out of your league and …"

"I suggest you mind your own business, Isobel."

The blonde woman grinned despite the not-so-subtle threat in his voice.

"You know me, Arthur. I never do."

SECOND CHANCES

Chapter 11

Arthur didn't approach the boy until the two women had
left the room. The extra time was as much for him to regain his
footing as for Matthew to get used to his presence. Isobel's
hints had pushed him out of his comfort zone. She had been
fishing of course, guessing that there was more to him and
Maya than met the eye, but she didn't know anything. Arthur
hoped he could trust Maya to resist the prodding.

The young man sat on the empty bed beside Matthew's
and loosened his tie, undoing one button from his collar. The
young boy was watching him closely.

During his last visit, Mark had overtaken Arthur's attention
so this was the first time he was able to really meet his charge.
The dark-haired boy had Maya's clear eyes, maybe a little
bluer, and a very delicate complexion, too delicate maybe. His
veins were an unmistakable blue web below his fair skin. The
tumor in his throat formed a small bump just below his Adam's
apple.

He had rarely seen a kid looking so fragile. His lips were
nearly purple with the lack of proper breathing; the low hiss of
his painful respiration was heart-breaking. Arthur wondered if
the boy would let him hold him the way he'd allowed Maya,
but something in the wary stare stopped him beforehand. Thus
he simply said, "Maya wants you to get better quickly."

The boy stayed still. Arthur relaxed his posture on the bed.

"I think that's because she really likes you."

This time a small grin rewarded his attempt. Arthur leaned
forward, his elbows on his knees, fingers linked.

"Are you afraid, Matthew?"

The direct question seemed to surprise the child and he didn't move right away. After a moment, he nodded once, slowly. Arthur stood up and went to sit on Matthew's bed, one leg folded over the rail, facing the boy.

"I understand. These tests will ensure that the doctors can safely remove that thing from your throat so you can have a normal life again."

He had always thought children understood a lot and were probably appalled by the dimwitted behavior of adults. As a kid, his father's severe attitude had contrasted a lot with the pitiful looks or suffocating coaxes. He had never fully understood why, but it had helped keep his head up. At times, he would have liked to be embraced like Maya did Matthew; but only his mother could have done that, and she was gone.

Matthew considered his explanation for an instant before he quietly slipped his little hand into the larger one and Arthur squeezed it. The little boy stirred the need to protect him in those around him and he could see why Maya was so taken with him. He briefly wondered how she would react if the surgery failed.

He smiled at the kid. He hoped with all his heart that it didn't.

*

After one hour of blind corridors, antiseptic scent and lectures about the hospital and the Foundation, Isobel asked for a truce. They stopped by the cafeteria for a cup of coffee. Maya picked up one for Arthur too, hoping he took his coffee with a cloud of milk.

"Wow, you even have him evolved from his bitter black espressos? You really have quite an influence on that guy, Maya."

She hid her embarrassment behind a cough. Why hadn't he taken the time to tell her that he took his coffee black and strong? Or whether he liked muffins? Damn him. How stupid of her to try to be nice and bring him a cup.

Apparently unaware of her sudden uneasiness, Isobel was looking at the other side of the room. She made a small noise with her tongue.

"Arthur is not my type but *he* definitely is ..."

Maya followed Isobel's stare and giggled.

"That is Gavin."

"I've heard that name before."

"Yes, probably from Colin."

The blonde sighed.

"Just my luck."

She pouted for a second before her laugher chimed once more and she grabbed Maya's arm, dragging her along.

"Since you stole my date, it's up to you to find me a suitable escort for the Yule Ball. Tall, dark, handsome, good dancer. Social and conversation skills are a nice addition but not mandatory."

Her description was cut short by the muffled sounds of an argument coming from the office nearby. Maya froze.

Moira's clear voice was answering a lower one, definitely male. Her sister was apparently having an argument with her fiancé. They were not that frequent, but rather nasty when they happened. Maya always avoided stepping in, especially when they shouted loud enough to be heard through the thick concrete walls. Unfortunately, the door opened before she could interest Isobel in the next wing.

"I am a member of the board, Moira, and I will look at those books. I don't need your permission!"

Tristan walked out, followed by a grunt of rage and the noise of a vase crashing on the floor. He ignored it. His handsome face was flushed with anger, which Maya didn't witness often. Tristan generally kept his cool, however distraught he was.

The young man ran one hand through his shoulder-length hair, breathing slowly to calm himself down, and smiled when he recognized the woman in front of him.

"Hi. I thought you were with Matthew this morning."

"We're going back there actually; Tristan, this is Isobel, the daughter of one of Robert's business partners. My cousin, Tristan Blois."

She hoped he had made the connection. Tristan answered the brilliant smile with a courteous bow, then excused himself. Isobel followed his retreat with an appreciative stare.

"Tell me he is not another one of Colin's friends."

Maya twitched her nose then her face lit up.

"No, no he is not. And he fulfills your requirements for a date very well, actually. What are you doing next Saturday?"

And just like that, the Christmas Market won another enthusiastic customer. Isobel was all too happy to escape her father and Robert for an entire day. Of course, it still left Arthur to be dealt with. But if she had to suffer his attentions, at least Isobel would help distract her cousin. Maya hoped Tristan wouldn't be too upset about her matchmaking attempt.

*

The ringing sound broke through the peaceful waiting room. Arthur reached for his pocket and sighed when he read

the name on the screen. Maya took the cell phone out of his
hand and flipped it open.

"I'm sorry, Robert. Arthur is busy right now."

Amazed, he watched her switch it off, before she slipped
the phone back in his hand without a sweat.

"Cell phones are not allowed inside the hospital."

Her tranquil smile was too much to take. Arthur scowled.

"Do you have any idea how my father is going to react to
that?"

"You said you were willing to take the risk."

Arthur couldn't recall when exactly she had begun
bouncing his own words back at him. It felt … good,
dangerous.

He pointed at Isobel, who was sipping her coffee while
looking through a window.

"How did it go?"

"Quite well, actually, she is very interesting. I've invited
her to join us on Saturday."

"You did what?!"

Concerned about his rising voice, Maya pressed one finger
on his lips to silence him. Arthur took it off immediately,
linking their fingers to make the gesture look natural. He
whispered, "We need to talk, Maya."

"Sure. Coffee?"

The horror on his face when he sipped her offering was
definitely worth whatever he had planned for a *conversation*.

SECOND CHANCES

Chapter 12

The tests lasted another hour before she was allowed to see Matthew. The boy was tired, and he refused to eat, falling asleep almost instantly once he was settled back in his bed. Maya tucked in the sheets around him and waited a few more minutes before going back to the cafeteria to grab some lunch.

Her sister was there, and she joined her. Moira's long blonde hair was hanging dully on her shoulders. Even pale and obviously tired, her sister was still a striking woman. Maya touched her shoulder gently before sitting next to her.

"Hi."

Moira jerked at the touch, her dark eyes searching the room frantically. Then she concentrated on her coffee again. Maya bit into her sandwich.

"Sorry. I didn't mean to startle you. Are you okay?"

"Yes, yes. I need a … I'm missing Cedric, that's all. He's been out of town for three days now."

Maya nodded and chewed quietly. She looked for something to say; Moira was very touchy lately, especially since Maya had begun *seeing* Arthur, and she had no desire to upset her further. The argument she had witnessed in the morning forbade discussing Tristan or even Isobel. Matthew and the Foundation were off limits too, for the subject would automatically bring up Arthur or Pendletons & Associates. Christmas holidays were a touchy subject because of their parents' disappearance.

It didn't leave a lot to discuss. Maya took another bite. Suddenly, it occurred to her she didn't have a lot in common with her older sister.

"I like your dress. Is it new?"

Maya looked up and grinned.

"Yes. Colin had a go at my wardrobe and convinced me to spend half of my salary on clothes."

"I'm glad you're finally wearing fitted clothes. You're very beautiful. At least this ridiculous affair seems to help you realize that."

Completely stunned, Maya glanced up. Moira's chocolate eyes were fervently scanning the room again. Could she really be missing her fiancé so much? It was unlike her sister to be that jittery, or even flattering. Moira generally gave orders more than compliments.

"I'm not beautiful."

"Don't be ridiculous, Maya, of course you are. Why you'd choose Arthur Pendleton when you could have any man is beyond me, though. He is so …"

The raven-haired woman held one hand up and her sister fell silent. The mention of her pseudo-boyfriend brought back the memory of one question Maya intended to ask.

"When I saw Robert yesterday evening …"

"I don't want to talk about Robert and his accusations."

How could Moira know Robert had accused them of anything? Maya insisted.

"Moira, what he implied …"

"I said I don't want to talk about him!"

Her voice rose as her temper flared. Maya sighed. This was another example of her older sister's volatile moods. She surprised herself by hoping Cedric would soon come back into town. At least when he was around, Moira looked happy, almost … ecstatic.

*

SECOND CHANCES

Leaving early one day, and spending the following morning entertaining a surprise guest had caused havoc to invade her office. The afternoon flew by quickly as Maya answered emails, phone calls, filed bills, and handled as much as she could in the very short amount of time left. Being Friday, she had to provide chores lists to the weekend teams, as well as prepare for the next week.

It had been dark for several hours already when she finally overcame the monstrous task of last-minute details with the organization for the upcoming Vallon Hospital Christmas Tree event.

Christmas was one of the busiest times for her, along with Thanksgiving and Halloween. This year, she had managed to convince Moira to plan the event for Christmas Eve, and the organization was worse in many ways. She had to contact every parent to make sure they planned their own celebration accordingly but also brought the presents in advance. She also had to book the team who would play Santa and his elves, and to deal with catering and temperamental decorators, unhappy to work on Christmas Eve. Right now, she felt as if her head was about to explode if she heard anything else about golden-winged angels and edible snowflakes.

Maya yawned and rubbed her tired eyes, instantly regretting it when she felt her contacts sliding. She blinked furiously several times to put them back in place, then closed her eyes and pressed her fingers to her lids to chase away the burning sensation. The sharp rap on her door forced her to use her eyes again.

"Come in."

She couldn't stop the sigh when she saw Arthur's tall figure entering the room. She had no desire to see him now; she just wanted to go home, to be blissfully alone and quiet.

"What are you doing here?"

He dismissed her rebuff with a wave of the hand.

"I promised Matthew to come back to see him after his tests were complete."

Her expression softened instantly. The nurse had called earlier to say the child had accepted mashed carrots, scrambled eggs and Jell-O for dinner. Arthur went on.

"He is sleeping. When will we receive the results?"

"Two or three days; if everything is positive, they will schedule the surgery for the end of next week, I hope."

Arthur nodded sternly. He stayed mute about the Yule Ball, which was happening the following weekend. The window behind her opened on the large square in front of the hospital. He approached to look at the white coat covering the sidewalks. Some flakes were whirling around; snow had started to fall again.

Maya stood up to distance herself from him. The young man looked from her open computer to her coat, hesitantly. He finally decided to help her with her clothing.

"If you're ready, I'll drive you home."

"Why?"

"I'm your boyfriend. Boyfriends do things like that on Friday nights, especially when it's dark and cold."

"You're not my boyfriend."

He only smirked. Maya bent to close her computer and Arthur turned his back on her, fishing for his keys.

Arthur had chosen the underground facility instead of parking in front of the building, and she appreciated not having to wait for the car to warm up. Of course, it was probably more for his convenience than hers, so Maya didn't thank him for it.

He turned left, exiting the garage and took the avenue leading downtown.

"Arthur, you're going west; my apartment is on the opposite side of the city."

"I know that. How do you feel about sushi?"

"Great, if you want to take me back to the hospital within the hour. I'm allergic to seafood, remember?"

The young man blushed deeply and fidgeted in his seat, uneasy.

"Sorry. It slipped my mind. Italian?"

"Can't you just bring me home?"

"Why do you refuse to have dinner with me? It's not like we can't stand each other."

Maya put her knitted fingers on her lap, looking straight ahead.

"We're not friends either."

"Do you have to be so difficult?"

"Do you have to be so stubborn?"

The only sign of impatience from Arthur came from his hand clenching the gearshift. Then, suddenly, he started laughing. Annoyed, Maya glared.

"What is so funny?"

"Well, I guess this was our first fight."

Her mouth twitched and the ghost of a smile blossomed on her lips. She renounced arguing. Truth was she was a little hungry and tired and escaping the cooking sounded good, even if it was Arthur's idea.

*

"This place is one of my favorites."

Curious, she inspected the small façade with red and green decorations. Arthur was already holding the door open.

"I think it's time we learn some things about each other."

"Well, you're stuck with milk in your coffee for a while."

His grimace widened her smile. Maya stepped inside the building, while his eyes burned holes in the back of her head.

The restaurant was an intimate little place, with white tablecloths and discreet waiters. Arthur chose a table near the fireplace. Maya had to admit he could be agreeable when he wanted to. He made some suggestions about the food, translating the menu for her, without making her feel out of place.

"I didn't know you speak Italian."

"I play golf too, but my Italian is better. *La signorina prenderà una zuppa con una scaloppina di vitello parmigiana e per me un carpaccio di bue con la scaloppina. Due bottiglie di acqua senza ghiaccio, con una fetta di limone.*"

The waiter took his order and left. Maya looked around before she focused on her companion again. Arthur sipped his drink.

"So, I take my coffee black, no sugar and I speak Italian. You're allergic to seafood. Even the score: tell me something about yourself."

She gave it a little thought before answering.

"Christmas is my favorite time of the year."

"I had guessed that. Tell me something else."

His blue eyes on her were unsettling. Suddenly the young woman realized the dinner looked a lot like a date, which was probably his intention from the beginning. Once again, Arthur was playing tricks on her. She could not trust him; his actions always hid ulterior motives.

"I live alone; I love children and I love my job at the Foundation; I play the piano; I love books and horror movies; I can't keep a plant alive for more than two months. I love live concerts. Is that enough for you?"

The avalanche of information was tinged with evident
annoyance. Arthur backed into his chair. He didn't understand
why she sounded angry all of a sudden. Her temper fuelled his
instantly.

"You forgot about your favorite dessert and animal."

"Raspberry sorbet and cats."

Their appetizers stopped the growing argument. They ate
in silence and the delicious food helped to settle their respective
flaring moods. Arthur put down his fork first.

"My turn, then. I visited Italy after college, and learned the
language. I speak bits of French too, mostly because I dated
women from the country. I used to play a lot of sports, but
lately I lack the time except for occasional indoor training. I
read so much during school I refuse to approach a book now. I
listen to whatever the radio is playing; I have never had a
relationship that lasted more than two weeks. I don't have
plants. I cannot remember the last time I took a proper
vacation. I like chocolate. No preference for cats or dogs."

Maya looked closely at him. Who defined oneself with so
many negations? Suddenly she doubted she knew who Arthur
Pendleton was, at all.

The food was incredible, and it helped finding a safer
conversation topic, as Maya asked Arthur to tell her about Italy.
She listened as he slowly opened up, talking about the beautiful
cities , Venice and Florence. He described the wonderful
buildings, the art and the *Dolce Vita,* and she discovered he
could be simple and passionate, a side of him that was new for
her and she actually liked. He still used irony to mock Italian
machismo, and exuberance, but he did it in a teasing way, to
amuse her rather than to vex.

"… Seriously, he could not be older than twelve. And here he was, parading and putting his sunglasses down his nose to wink at women twice his age. And it worked!"

"They were probably making fun of him."

Arthur shook his head.

"No, not at all. Believe me, I know when a woman is interested or not."

Maya opened her mouth to retort she had no doubt about it, but closed it again. Arthur noticed her hesitation and fell silent, his grin vanishing quickly. Their waiter arrived to clear their dishes; both welcomed the interruption.

"May I bring you some dessert? Coffee?"

Maya shook her head.

"Oh, no, thank you. I could not swallow another bit. It was delicious."

"Caffe dopio per me."

"Si signore."

Casual conversation seemed no longer an option. Maya sipped her water. She regretted holding her tongue earlier. Maybe Arthur would have understood she was teasing, and just joked back. He was glimpsing toward the kitchens, probably hoping for his double espresso to arrive as soon as possible. She sighed. No, Arthur ignored self-derision. Teasing his dating habits would have been equally disastrous. So be it. She had questions, and he was already antagonized …

"I still don't understand why you can't simply say no to Robert about his marital ideas instead of all this machination."

Arthur reacted instantly.

"You don't know what it's like to deal with a man who does not consider 'no' as a suitable answer."

She did not; but she could guess well enough. Be successful; be flawless; obey blindly. She'd had her share when she was younger, when she was in high school and Robert still cared about the whereabouts of his goddaughter.

Their waiter presented Arthur with his coffee and left. She watched her companion more closely as he spooned his coffee unnecessarily – his stare fixed on the dark beverage, sailing away already. Maya refused to let him close up so she teased, "You could do worse than Isobel. At least she is nice."

After a moment, Arthur looked up. His expression was mocking again and she dreaded his response.

"You surprise me, Maya. You, of all people, approving of arranged unions?"

Maya tensed. "I don't–"

"No, of course you don't. You are a romantic at heart."

She frowned.

"If I was that romantic, I would get caught in this masquerade, fall helplessly in love with you, and nurse a broken heart for the rest of my life."

Arthur laughed and gestured for the bill.

"Fortunately for your tender heart, this has little chance of happening, right?"

She liked his tone less and less and replied dryly.

"Absolutely."

"Then we're good."

Arthur drained his coffee and stood to proceed to the cashier.

Maya followed his retreat, speechless. She nearly swore he sounded sad.

SECOND CHANCES

Chapter 13

Maya turned to look at the clock on her bedside table. It was barely eight. She stretched, arching her back and curling her toes, before rolling on her stomach to bury her face in the pillow. She could indulge a bit longer in the warm bed; Tristan would not arrive for at least another hour and Arthur had announced he would join them directly at the market. She suspected he was going to the office, even though he had not disclosed any reason for his delay.

She sighed and flipped on her back again, disturbed by memories of their dinner. From his own confessions, Arthur was a workaholic, and he settled for undemanding getaways when he had some free time, which was apparently very rare. Colin seemed to be his only real friend. Somehow, she pitied him.

Knowing this, their little masquerade was gathering a new meaning. By refusing his father's choice for a daughter-in-law, he was shaking the stifling cloak cast over him; or at least he was trying to escape it. She pondered if Arthur was even conscious of his attempt. Probably not.

Restless, Maya pushed away the sheets and walked to the bathroom. Arthur's true motives for asking her to pose as his girlfriend were his and his alone and they would remain so.

As for her, all that mattered was Matthew … and for the next couple of hours, preventing her 'suitor' and her cousin from killing each other. Of course, Isobel was going to help by distracting Tristan, or so she hoped.

She had yet to tell her cousin they were to have company for the day. She was nearly sure he would not object to Isobel, but Arthur was another matter. Maya twisted her hair into a bun and observed her image in the mirror. Moira's comment the previous day came back to taunt her. Her sister was seeing her with biased eyes. She was far from being beautiful. Interesting, maybe, but certainly not anything more than that. She sighed and smiled, dismissing the thought, then turned the hot water on to have a shower.

*

Tristan took a mouthful of coffee.

"Did I miss something?"

"Huh, no. That's it. We will pick up Isobel at her hotel and Arthur will join us later."

He gulped more coffee.

"Why?"

"Arthur argued he had to come because we are supposed to be together and I can't be seen spending my weekend with another man, even you."

"Right. But what about Isobel? Arthur didn't require her presence, I suppose. Isn't she Robert's choice for a daughter-in-law?"

Talking about Isobel was exactly what Maya had hoped to avert. Unfortunately, her cousin knew her too well to let her off the hook that easily. She tried to smile her way out of it.

"I like her?"

He pointed one accusatory finger at her and repeated, "Right. Try again, Maya."

"Oh fine! She needs a date for the Yule Ball because I'll go with Arthur, and I thought that if you like each other …"

Tristan choked on his beverage, his cheeks growing a deep pink.

"I beg your pardon?"

Maya gave him her best kitty-cat pout.

"Maya ..."

"Oh, please Tristan. You've been pining over Ines for too long now. You deserve a little fun. Isobel is nice and attractive and she's ..."

Her mention of his former girlfriend shadowed his face instantly and she regretted bringing up the name. Tristan groaned.

"I don't have a choice, I suppose."

She beamed and leaned over to kiss his cheek.

"I'm sure you'll like her."

Tristan interrupted her at once.

"I warn you, Maya. This is not an invitation for you to try to pair me up, and make sure your 'date' stays away from me. Is that clear?"

"Crystal!"

She danced out of the kitchen and the young man sighed heavily, vaguely suspicious about the trouble she was leading him into. He equally worried about the reasons that had pushed Maya to play matchmaker. In his experience, she did that only when her loving heart was content. He drained the rest of his coffee. Spending the day watching Arthur Pendleton was probably a good thing.

*

"Oh, my, these are fantastic!"

Isobel tugged Maya toward the next shop to admire the homemade knitted pieces. Maya smiled in apology at her cousin as her nose, pink with cold, disappeared behind layers of forest green wool. The cloth was incredibly soft on her skin and she rubbed the fabric against her cheek while Isobel chose another one and giggled. The bright yellow piece made its way back on the rack. The blonde woman wrapped a fuchsia scarf around her, then a cornflower blue one and a gray, admiring herself in the small mirror nearby.

Tristan observed them from afar for a minute before he started moving slowly toward them. Isobel radiated energy and charm and her bright smile was contagious. His cousin tended to be reserved with strangers, but the blonde had overcome her shyness without Maya even knowing it. His stare found a pair of intelligent gray eyes, and Isobel's smile widened, before it turned slightly mischievous. Her gaze fixed on him and sparkled.

"Tristan, come here."

The young man obeyed, praying she didn't make him try on the pink scarf, or the yellow one. Isobel took off the dark gray scarf from herself to enfold it around his neck. The wool was already imprinted with her scent, some light touch of orchids and amaranth wood. The instant desire to discover more surprised him and he accepted it heartily, while she played with the scarf. She had to rise up on her toes to arrange it and maybe she leaned on him a little more than strictly required. Tristan wondered if she tasted of plums and roses, as sweet as she looked. Maya had been right. Isobel was attractive; very very attractive.

The raven-haired woman grinned behind her bundle of wool: Isobel had Tristan under her charm, and he seemed more than happy to go under. Maya tried to untangle the scarf Isobel had tied around her neck, twisting her arms to reach the knot behind her head. A gloved hand brushed the tape of her neck and she flinched as cold air rushed under the now loose scarf.

"You should buy it; the color suits you."

Arthur made no move toward her and Maya stayed disconcerted for a second. Suspicion kicked in and warmed her cheeks lightly despite the icy wind. He wanted *her* to kiss *him* first, and not the other way around. Surely his attitude was custom-made to enrage Tristan.

Sadist.

She folded the scarf scrupulously, refusing to play his game without at least challenging him, so one brow quirked up.

"Aren't you forgetting something, Arthur?"

He grinned and Maya didn't know what to make of his smile, a tease or real good humor.

"Of course."

Ha!

"Where are my manners? Good morning, Isobel."

He brushed the blonde's cheek swiftly while Tristan glared. Maya fought the urge to stab Arthur with something really sharp, and she mentally kicked herself for it. He was saving her the embarrassment of a meaningless kiss, and so she should be grateful, not ... *Hell of a man.*

Isobel spared her the humiliation of kicking him in the knee, or higher if she could reach.

"Arthur stop looking at her like she's some forbidden fruit. Are you an item or not? Just kiss her."

Isobel turned toward the clerk, and her bargain disappeared in the drums of his heart pounding when he obeyed and pressed one light kiss on her lips.

Her skin was cold from the outdoors and warm at the same time. Like their previous kisses, the caress fired more need deep within him and Arthur had to fight to step back. Avoiding her blazing stare, he turned toward Tristan and offered his hand.

"Hey, sorry to be late."

Tristan hesitated, looking from the offered hand to the calm face of his nemesis. Isobel was already eyeing the next store, a pottery shop Maya was dying to visit too.

"I sure could use some help…"

"Great."

A brief nod in addition to the handshake sealed the truce.

*

Maya perused the figurines. She loved the precious carvings from this particular shop, and the previous year she had bought the basics of her crèche: Mary and the infant Jesus, and Joseph. Tristan had offered her the traditional ox and donkey to complete the set. This year, she was looking forward to adding the magi and shepherds.

Unfortunately, none were on display. The artisan confirmed he had not brought any for this year's Market, for the holy scene was becoming less and less popular. He suggested she check his catalog, but she refused, disappointed. Isobel cut in with some questions about faience techniques for she was an amateur in pottery herself.

Maya turned her back to the little sculptures of clay to examine painted plates and jars and Tristan slipped one arm around her shoulders.

"He doesn't have your magi, hum?"

"Nope. Maybe next year."

"Why don't you order them?"

"It's not the same thing."

He nudged her chin gently with two fingers. Maya rested against her cousin, enjoying the comfort a moment, before she asked.

"So … What do you think of Isobel?"

Tristan wrinkled his nose.

"She's terrible; I don't want to see her ever again."

Maya laughed.

"Liar."

"Don't push your luck. Let's go for lunch, and we'll find your excuse of a Christmas tree afterward."

The cousins gestured to their friends, who were still talking to the merchant, and stepped out into the cold again.

*

The Christmas Market was composed of several little barracks shaped like Swiss Chalets, with exposed wooden beams and red sloping gables. The snow gave it a joyful glow, especially with the music pouring from speakers attached to poles in the alleys. Each chalet had a portable heater attached to the roof, so customers could shop comfortably.

The Market, like every year, had been installed in one of the biggest esplanades of the city. For the occasion, the cafés in the arcades surrounding the square had reopened their terraces, with the same heating concept, and they chose one that overlooked the ice rink created for the holidays.

Isobel clapped her hands cheerfully.

"Oh, I want to skate after lunch."

Maya nodded more quietly.

"Sure, why not."

Tristan poked at her.

"Are you sure? Last time you tried you ended up with nasty bruises."

She frowned.

"It was your fault. You pushed me when I was not ready."

"You skate like a penguin, Maya. You're so stiff it's a wonder you don't hurt yourself more badly."

She stuck out her tongue at Tristan who laughed.

"Just admit you can't skate, just like you can't ride a horse."

"I have no problem with horses."

"What is it about horses?" Arthur asked.

He vaguely recalled she had always skipped the riding lessons as a child. His father was a hard coach; he thought at the time she resented his methods. He was personally a proficient rider.

Maya answered quickly.

"Nothing."

Tristan contradicted her, to her greatest displeasure.

"She's afraid of falling."

"Am not."

"Get over it, Maya. It's not that dramatic."

"I can ride a horse."

Isobel diverted the conversation, sensing the other girl was getting upset with the unrelenting teasing.

Maya appreciated her new friend's tact and they finished their meal happily.

Afternoon was already half gone by the time they left the small café to join the skaters. Daylight was already fading and the air grew colder. Tristan and Isobel went in scouting; the blonde woman was hanging on his arm and the white little clouds created by their chatting in the icy air entwined with each other.

Arthur stopped Maya when she tried to follow.

"Matthew's wish is about horses, isn't it?"

Of course he had made the connection. She gritted her teeth.

"Yes."

Maya hoped he understood and dropped the subject. She started walking but he restrained her again. Annoyed, she had no choice but to face him.

"I gave my word I'll take him for a ride after he is healed from his operation. And I will."

Her clear eyes shone fiercely before she turned away. Arthur grabbed her arm as if to escort her.

"I'll help."

"You don't have to. Your part will be finished by then."

"I know. I'll help."

She launched her arms around his neck. The spontaneous hug unsettled him, but it ended (too) quickly. Maya smiled at him and took his hand to lead him toward their friends. Isobel's piercing stare felt even more annoying than the goofy grin he feared he had on his face.

*

Arthur shook his head when the rink employee turned to him to ask his shoe-size. Maya looked up to him, abandoning temporarily the unlacing of her boots.

"You are not skating?"

"No, not this time; I have a feeling the spectacle is going to be much more enjoyable from the stage."

Tristan frowned at his teasing tone. Maya made a face at Arthur and returned to her preparation.

Isobel was pirouetting on the ice long before Maya had completed fixing her first skate. Her cousin patted her knee before he got up.

"Just take it easy, okay? We are not in a hurry."

"Yes of course. I won't be long."

She smiled beautifully at Tristan and the young man joined Isobel. Arthur had followed the exchange without a word, looking at the blonde rotating gracefully in the center of the ring. He glanced back at Maya. She was done with her second blade, and putting her gloves back on before standing up.

Arthur backed from the rink, looking for a seat. The young woman stood and slowly started toward the border. He plunged his hands deep in his coat's pockets. The hint of anxiety when she had answered her cousin was now reflecting on her face. She was a little pale, despite the touch of pink the cold had brought to her cheeks. How easily he started to read her emotions was unnerving.

Maya eyed the gleaming surface with a defiant look. Isobel waved at them.

"Are you coming? The ice is just perfect!"

She gave a hand back and answered "Coming!"

Nearby, the cheer did not sound so joyful. Maya took one hesitant step forward. On an impulse, Arthur grabbed her arm as her other hand crisped on the rim.

"You don't have to go if you don't feel like it."

Her surprised stare left the ice to his gloved hand circling her biceps, then his face. Arthur released his grip immediately, vaguely annoyed with his reaction. She made it too easy to let things be, to forget about everything and just enjoy the moment. He did not like seeing her wary. He felt concerned for her, and the feeling made him ill at ease.

A stubborn pout twisted her lips.

"I want to skate."

"Yes, that's crystal clear."

His sarcasm fired her temper instantly.

"At least I make an effort to enjoy myself."

Arthur took one step forward and she backed, sliding on the ice. Her hands shot to the wall to steady herself.

"You are not enjoying yourself, Maya, you are being stubborn. You are going to hurt yourself."

"No I will not."

She moved forward on the ice, testing its surface; her arms stretched behind her, and he noticed their trembling. His stomach clenched uncomfortably. Arthur wondered if he could simply grab her to take her to the safety of the ground. She would probably flog him if he did, if she did not slap him. He barely understood why he wanted to do that. Maya spoke again.

"Tristan likes to skate, and Isobel seems to like it too."

"Let them enjoy it together, then. Clearly, they are having fun on their own."

Her cousin and Isobel were sliding side by side at the center of the rink, laughing. Maya grinned, then gasped when suddenly a teen brushed by her on his mad race with his friends. Forgetting their growing argument, she worked her arms like springs to approach the wall again, tightening her grasp on her support. Her obstinacy started to annoy him for good. He moved away to sit on the bench she had used to lace her skates.

"Very well, then. Show me your skills."

Despite her obvious irritation at the patronizing tone, her hands stayed glued to the wall.

"Why don't *you* join us, Arthur?"

There was no way he was going to tell her *he* did not know how to skate. He smirked instead.

"Seeing you stumbling to stay up is much more fun."

Maya glared. She opened her mouth to answer, when his cell phone rang. Arthur peeked at the number on display, and sighed. On a Saturday afternoon, the office's call could come only from his father.

"I have to take this; please excuse me."

When he ended his call, Maya had joined Tristan and Isobel at the center of the rink. Isobel held both her hands and was trying to show her how to relax on her blades. By the stiffness in Maya's body language, it would take more than one lesson.

Chapter 14

Arthur pressed his fingers to his temples. Maya had apparently very personal ideas about what a Christmas tree should be, and she was determined to find it. The systematic refusal of her friends' suggestions was getting on his nerves. Her stubbornness had a glint that reminded him a little too much of his father. As a matter of fact, each denial was growing into the familiar headache his father's demeanour frequently caused.

Tristan looked resigned. Apparently, he knew his pigheaded cousin well enough not to interfere. Isobel kept trying, although Arthur wondered why, being that each unsuccessful (and seemingly unwelcome) suggestion was dismissed rather quickly. At least while she helped Maya busying herself with those stupid pines, Isobel was not looking at him with that pensive pout he associated with doubts.

Arthur took a couple of steps back to take in some fresh air and clear his head.

"No, I prefer a small tree."

"What about this one?"

"Too plump."

Isobel was about to show her another one but Tristan stopped her.

"Believe me, it's simpler to let her choose for herself."

"But …"

"Anything you will point out she is going to refuse. Let her. Will you share dinner with us tonight?"

The blonde woman smiled sweetly. Of course, Maya had already invited her, but she kept it to herself.

"I'd like that."

Tristan brushed imaginary needles off her coat, playing with the golden locks.

"Great."

She got up on her toes to meet him midway for a first kiss when Maya called from afar.

"Found it!"

Tristan straightened up with a sigh. Isobel chuckled and cupped his face, pulling him back to her.

"Not so fast, handsome."

Arthur detached his attention from his father's last text-message at the call. Turning to see if Tristan and Isobel could handle it, he spotted them under a bunch of mistletoe. Apparently, their passionate kissing left him with the task of finding Maya and her tree. Trust Isobel to add to his burden every chance she had.

Maya was already bargaining with the clerk to save her treasure.

"I'll take this one."

Arthur bent his head to the side.

"Are you sure?"

She frowned at the doubtful tone.

"Yes, I'm sure. It's my tree and I want this one."

Arthur held his hand to stop the coming argument.

"Fine. I'll bring the car."

Isobel and Tristan saw him walk stiffly out of the garden center and walked toward Maya. Isobel wrapped one arm around her waist.

"Is everything alright? Arthur looks a bit … dissatisfied."

She shrugged her shoulders, already opening her mouth to say that Arthur's mood was none of her concerns. Tristan sensed the danger and pointed at the tree.

"Isn't it... crooked?"

The word was an understatement. Pitiful or ridiculous would have been a better assessment of her choice. The poor tree was asymmetrical with an overgrown head and branches twisted into some impossible shape instead of the proper pyramid. He tried to imagine it covered with the decorations. The picture didn't help. Tristan sighed, stoical.

"If you like it..."

Maya beamed.

"Yes, it's perfect."

Minutes later, they had the tree settled in the back of Arthur's SUV. To Maya's displeasure, she had no choice but to climb in with him, while Tristan and Isobel followed in the second car.

The easiness that had followed his offering of help with Matthew's wish and her impromptu thanks was long gone. Arthur focused on the road, while she looked through her window.

With the fallen night, bands of fog were invading the streets, giving the city a ghostly aspect she loved.

"Haunting."

Arthur glimpsed at her.

"Sorry, what?"

"Tonight's movie. I want to see something about haunting and ghosts."

"As you wish."

His lack of interest galled her and she closed her arms over her chest.

"You don't have to stay if you don't want to."

"Actually, my father sent me a message about some papers he needs for his negotiations with Isobel's father."

Maya reacted instantly.

"Arthur, it's Saturday night!"

"It doesn't matter. Plus, it's the perfect excuse for me to go. If you can pout long enough, Isobel will simply lecture me for abandoning you, and the illusion will stand. It will even allow us some time apart without too much suspicion."

"You have clearly figured out every detail."

One eyebrow shot up at the bitterness in her voice, but he said nothing. After a while, Maya spoke again.

"I suggest you just drop me at my place and go. I'm perfectly able to make it look like a real dispute as it is."

Arthur acquiesced, indifferent. Why she sounded angry was beyond him.

*

The door squeaked and Arthur lifted his head to see his father enter his office. Robert was wearing his tuxedo, a sign he was on his way to the opera or the theatre, or rather coming back from it given the time on the clock.

"I didn't expect to find you here, Arthur."

'As if you hadn't texted me about those minor adjustments *you needed ASAP.'*

Arthur kept his face scrupulously devoid of emotion as Robert settled into one of the chairs in front of the desk.

"I hoped Maya was not too upset about your… getaway."

The word was carefully chosen and spilled with enough contempt to make the hair on his neck bristle.

"Yes, she was."

'Surprisingly.'

"Maya tends to let her emotions dictate her decisions. You will find a way to smooth her ruffled feathers, I trust."

Arthur liked the conversation less and less by the second. The way his father talked about his ward was disturbing at best; abusive. First, because Robert had loved her deeply; and second, because Arthur didn't really need his mind to venture in some particularly intriguing directions more than it already did.

He turned to pick up some sheets from the printer behind him and handed them to his father.

"Your addenda."

Robert barely took a look at the notes before he discarded them.

"What did you learn about the Foundation?"

There they were.

"Nothing we didn't know. Without tangible proof, we can't do more than block their account. I'm not expecting the commission to give its approval for a financial verification anytime soon because of the holidays."

"Call the judge. Of course, he'll need a detailed list of their bank operations to proceed."

Arthur froze. Such information was confidential. Only the members of the Foundation's board and their accountant had access to that. His father was suggesting (not asking, of course not – Robert would never assume responsibility for such an act – that he used his 'connection' to Maya to access the information. Such a 'suggestion' was borderline illegal, besides unethical. Again.

The young man composed himself before he answered slowly.

"I suppose such data could help find out if the dealers are using the Foundation to launder some cash."

Dissatisfied with the answer, Robert narrowed his eyes and Arthur held the glacial stare. After a couple of seconds, the older man broke the eye contact and stood, smoothing his white silk scarf.

Arthur swallowed.

"Father, I don't think Maya knows anything about the drugs. She doesn't know Moira is ..."

"Of course. She's way too naïve." Robert smirked. "And indeed she is, to believe you're truly in love with her."

Arthur counted up to twenty before he allowed himself to release his grip on the armchair after the door closed, breathing deeply. The immobility helped relax the tension in his stomach, and the pounding in his head decreased accordingly. Some days, the heartless businessman hardly looked like his father, a man who deserved his respect, and his affection. Arthur switched off the lights and walked out of his office.

Passing by the giant Christmas tree at the entrance of the building, he wondered what Maya's tree looked like. It was very late to find out.

Chapter 15

Her glasses lay on the floor, between the sofa and the coffee table. The anchorman on TV announced the weather forecast and Maya yawned, annoyed to have missed more than half of her movie.

She yawned again and snuggled on the couch, reluctant to move. If she was to sleep, her bed would be far more comfortable but the blanket was agreeably warm…

The buzz finally caught her attention. Maya stood and walked to the door to answer, shivering.

"Who's there?"

"Arthur."

Reproaches for bothering her so late died on her tongue at the sight of him, and she pulled him in without a word. Arthur sank into a chair and let his head fall back on the cushion, eyes closed.

"Are you alright? You look …"

"Just a headache."

Asking if he needed some aspirin sounded lame. She proposed food instead.

"I'm not hungry. Thanks."

At a loss for what to do or say, Maya wrapped her blanket around her shoulders and folded her long legs under her. Arthur opened his eyes to look around. Her apartment was the same, still small and cramped. *Cozy.*

"Your tree is weird."

"Tristan said 'horrible'."

Tristan had said horrible and Isobel had tactfully avoided describing the poor thing. She smiled at the memory. Arthur closed his eyes again.

"Your cousin has no taste."

His comment was clearly meant to irritate her but Maya grinned sweetly.

"Isobel would object to that."

"See what I mean?"

"Why are you here, Arthur?"

He glanced up. The dark blue stare was devoid of the usual mocking gleam. What glittered in his eyes was something else, lassitude or longing. Troubled, Maya repeated softly:

"Why are you here?"

Arthur turned his head, considering the tree again, or looking for the proper words to answer.

"I don't know."

He truly didn't. The confrontation with his father had left him empty, and sick. Returning to his place had seemed like a colossal task he had not had the strength to pursue. Suddenly, he had craved for softness and innocence, rather than the solace of loneliness and bourbon, and he had ended up on her doorstep. Right now, with her liquid eyes searching his face, the alcohol seemed a better idea.

Arthur got up.

"I have to go."

"Arthur …"

"I'll call you. Good night."

Maya stared at the door for a long time after it closed behind him. She trusted that Arthur coldly calculated his every move in their *relationship*. So why was her heart murmuring something about delusion and second chances?

*

Tristan rapped on the door and passed his head through the half-opening. The young woman gestured for him to enter, the receiver jammed below her jaw as she typed furiously on her keyboard.

"No, Arthur, not yet... Yes, I'll let you know... Yes... Bye."

She put the phone back into place, pressed a couple more keys, and then looked up at her cousin.

"Hello."

"Hi. What's with the frenzy?"

Maya pushed one strand of hair from her face.

"The catering service wants to trade gingerbread and cupcakes for something with carrots, and the agency suddenly decided they need half of the amount in advance for the puppets."

He pouted.

"I totally object about the carrots."

"So did I. But they're not happy. The cook lectured me for twenty minutes about nutrition and health care. They do that all the time, I'm starting to think we will hire another caterer next time."

"I guess having Arthur on your back for whatever he was asking is not really helpful either."

Maya smiled up her sleeve. The two men had apparently agreed on a truce of some sort the previous Saturday, yet it didn't mean Tristan had completely forgotten the past. She twisted her neck to relax the tension there, tired.

"He just wanted to know if Matthew's test results were back. It's nice of him to call."

His fingers drummed on his knee absently.

"I suppose. Anyway, I didn't come to talk about Arthur. "

Maya frowned as her computer beeped to announce a new email had arrived.

"Is there something wrong?"

"I don't know yet."

More drumming. Maya abandoned her work to stare at her cousin.

"I contacted the bank."

"Really? Why didn't you check the account through the system?"

Ill at ease, Tristan straightened up in his chair.

"I didn't want Moira to find out. I think she knows full well what's wrong with the Foundation."

"Of course not, how can you say that!"

"Maya ..."

"Just because the two of you had a fight, it doesn't mean she's guilty of something! She was sad because Cedric was away, that's all!"

Tristan sighed, looking for another angle to explain.

"Didn't you notice she is more and more of a lunatic every day? Or that she has lost some weight?"

"She works a lot."

"So do you, but you don't automatically have a fight with whomever walks your way."

"Sometimes I do."

He insisted.

"There's a problem with Moira, and you know it."

She couldn't believe Tristan was saying such things. She *didn't want* to believe he was.

Robert had said to ask Moira about the finances. Now Tristan believed there was something wrong with her sister. Robert she didn't care about, but Tristan she did. He was the practical one; he looked at things with objectivity, never jumping to conclusions without thinking it through.

Maya glanced away. As much as she didn't want to believe him, deep down she knew her cousin was right.

"Will you let me know what you find? Please?"

"Of course I will."

Tristan walked around the desk to take her into his arms. The young woman let him hug her, her nose lost in his shoulder, seeking some comfort for the difficulties to come.

A cheerful voice interrupted them.

"Maya, tell me you're not trying to steal another man from me."

Grinning, she circled her cousin's neck with both arms and kissed his jaw noisily.

"Oh I don't know ... Tall, dark, handsome, good dancer, well-bred; I might."

Isobel laughed.

"You're not that annoyed with Arthur, darling. Plus, you'll need my help with your dress."

*

Maya smoothed the fabric on her hips, looking at her image in the mirror of the small changing room. The movement wrinkled the velvet, which shone softly. The dress was lovely.

Isobel called through the curtain.

"So, what do you think?"

"It's nice."

"Then you need to try another one."

She sighed. Her friend had said exactly the same thing twice already. She loved the three dresses, this one, the red silk, and the blue satin. The blue gown neckline was so low she blushed just looking at herself in the mirror. The red dress clung to her curves in such a way that she was feeling nearly naked, and incredibly powerful. If she knew Arthur's favorite color, it would be easier.

Maya chastised herself. Arthur's liking was not the point, absolutely not.

"What color is your dress, Isobel?"

"Light green, with a touch of gray."

Gray and green meant the one she was wearing at the moment was out of the question. Maya nibbled at her upper lip, hesitant. One hand appeared above the door.

"Try this one."

Isobel's choice was white and seemed to catch every ray of light to transform them into gold. The fabric was light, marvellously soft and bright.

"You look like an angel…"

The embellished one-shoulder strap wrapped the fabric so it formed closely to her chest and left her shoulders bare. She whirled and the skirt flowed around her legs like water. The ankle-length skirt was slit up the thigh on one side. Maya laughed.

"I don't feel like one."

The gray eyes fixed on her gleamed with mischief and Isobel winked.

"Even better. Poor Arthur will never know what hit him."

Maya stopped playing with her skirt. Isobel poked her arm.

"Come on, Maya, I know a set-up when I see one."

She swallowed, unsure if she should deny it or just admit the truth.

Isobel winked and left the dressing room to let her change, grinning and grabbing the dismissed dresses to hand the items back to the clerk. Her friends were fooling themselves just as much as they were fooling Robert and the rest of the world. She knew Arthur well enough to notice his behavior around Maya was different; his guard was down and he acted less harshly, as if he *cared*. Maya was harder to read, but there was something in her way of accepting Arthur around her, in her blushes and in her smiles, which spoke volumes about what her reaction would be if Arthur tried to charm her *for real*. As to whether or not one sexy dress was going to be enough for them to accept it...

SECOND CHANCES

Chapter 16

The little boy looked even frailer than the previous week, Arthur thought. His eyes shone abnormally bright, and they seemed to have sunk deeper into their sockets. He pushed away from the door when the nurse approached holding the lunch tray.

Arthur stopped her.

"Give me that."

The woman tiredly handed him her load, not even waiting for him to enter, and went on with her tasks. The child was crouched in his bed. Arthur sat near him and smiled.

"Hi, Matthew."

The little boy moved a little to give him more space. Arthur lifted the cover and frowned. The meal included cubes of ham and rice with sweet-peas; all of which the kid could clearly not swallow. He took the plastic fork and mashed the peas the best he could.

"Here ..."

Matthew hesitantly took a half-spoon of vegetables. The effort of swallowing the hard and dry food made the clear blue eyes water, and the child nestled back against Arthur without a second attempt at eating. The young man pushed the dark hair back to kiss his burning forehead.

"I know it hurts, Matthew, but you have to eat to get better."

The little boy shook his head and buried his face deeper into his chest to sob. Pushing the tray away, Arthur enfolded his charge in his arms, gently caressing his head to quieten him.

"Well, peas are not fun, I'll give you that."

While Matthew calmed down in his embrace, he looked around. The other bed was empty; Mark was finally home with his family. Some books were stacked up on the bedside table; all about horses. He picked one and opened it at the bookmark, undoubtedly left by Maya.

Pain half-forgotten, Matthew looked at him with pleading eyes. Arthur grinned.

"I am going to make a deal with you. You drink the milk and eat some of your dessert, and we'll read one chapter."

"Do you really need to negotiate everything, Arthur?"

Maya entered with another tray. Matthew wriggled to free himself from Arthur to get to her and she embraced the little boy heartily. The young man stood so she could take his place near the child on the bed.

"I do not."

"Milk and dessert for one chapter? That's bargaining to me."

Smiling, she uncovered a bowl of soup, mashed sweet potatoes and a small bowl of chocolate mousse. Matthew's nose twitched at the smell of the food and his eyes lit with pleasure.

The brutal desire to possess forever the wonderful picture of Maya with the child cuddled in her arms punched him hard in the stomach. Arthur inhaled deeply to repress the feeling, looking away and settling in the farthest chair he could find.

"Go on, Arthur, read. We'll eat."

Her teasing smile awoke more needs. She was impossible. But Matthew was sipping his soup. So he read.

*

Maya pulled the door behind them as the little boy turned in his sleep.

"The surgery is scheduled on the thirtieth, but I'm not sure he can wait that long."

The worry in her voice was unmistakable and he found he wanted to reach for her; so he chose another question to distract himself from the need.

"Why don't they feed him intravenously instead of forcing him to eat normally?"

"Gavin told me it's better to keep his digestive system working for as long as possible. He said it will help later with the rehabilitation."

Some hair had escaped her braid, and she pushed it off her face. Arthur noticed the shadows under her eyes; she was tired. He concentrated on their conversation again.

"He clearly couldn't swallow the food on his tray. Why …"

"The service made a mistake when Mark checked out. Do you see this number here?"

She twisted to point to the small number on the cover of the first tray and her movement stretched her blouse. Arthur peeped at the writing above her shoulder and withdrew quickly. Her scent and the view were unnerving.

"28-B."

"That's the number of Mark's bed. Matthew is 28-A. They delivered the wrong one. I talked to Moira about it but she's …"

"Distracted."

The word came out before he could stop himself. Maya gave him an astonished look then turned away.

"Yes. I need to talk to my assistant about the trays. I won't be long."

111

Arthur nodded and entered her office to wait. Suddenly, coming by on his lunch hour to see Matthew seemed like a bad idea. He should not have given in to the impulse. He had a lot to do before leaving the next day. His father was on his back for the Mercia contract and the Foundation's case, and he was wasting time waiting for a woman; for Maya.

The screen saver on her computer screen was wishing him a Merry Christmas. Arthur sat on her chair, glancing at the other items on her desk; one pen was missing its cover; she had obviously played with it. A to-do list for the day was scribbled on a Post-it.

His gaze kept coming back to the computer. All he had to do was to move the mouse to access her account. With one click or two, he could find the information they needed to clear the Foundation.

The photo near the monitor showed a middle-aged man with two girls clutched to his neck, a blonde and a brunette. The girls seemed to be laughing their hearts out, obviously trying to bring the man down on the grass: Gerald, Moira and Maya, years ago, when things were not so complicated.

Arthur looked back at the screen. Drugs hurt millions of people, most likely Moira too. Bringing down one financial resource would not stop the traffic but it would certainly make things a bit more difficult for the dealers to dispatch their Evil. Cutting resources was like burning the legendary Hydra head: it didn't kill the monster but it prevented the severed head from growing twice as powerful. He extended his hand.

"What are you doing?"

The ruffled tone stopped him midway to the mouse. Arthur backed up in her chair slowly, while his mind was working in overdrive to find a suitable explanation. She would not believe him. She didn't trust him, yet she trusted everybody else... She was too trusting for her own good, far too innocent. *If* she was innocent...

"I was bored."

The half-lie, voiced with one touch of contempt, instantly appalled her. Temper flared in her pale green eyes.

"Well, surely you can find … amusement elsewhere."

God, she was beguiling when she was mad. Standing, Arthur smirked.

"You're selling yourself short, sweetheart. I'll pick you up at your place tomorrow, two o'clock sharp. Don't forget your toothbrush."

He crushed her into him, utterly (dis)satisfied when she turned her head so his mouth found only her jaw, because he had expected her to react exactly like that. As long as he could predict her reactions, and he kept his under control, he would be safe.

*

Maya checked her bag for the thirtieth time. Her outfit for the Ball and a change of clothes were carefully stored in a small suitcase, as well as her toothbrush and toiletries. She had changed her choice of nightgown three times already. Each one was perfectly decent; plain.

"Don't be ridiculous, Maya, this is not a romantic getaway, it's business."

Even speaking the reality out loud didn't help. She threw the garment she was holding into the bag and zipped it up before she changed her mind again. The nightdress was green. Arthur had said green suited her. She couldn't take the green one!

Maya was about to reopen her luggage when the door buzzed. It was too late to change her mind now. She took a deep breath, checked her reflection in the mirror, mentally kicking herself for it, and opened the front door.

He was wearing jeans. It was the first time she had seen him without a tailored suit since they had started their charade. He looked good in jeans. The navy color of his pullover matched his eyes. He had not tied his scarf and the skin of his neck was pink with cold.

"Hi."

The syllable choked and Maya felt like an idiot.

"Let me take that."

Without hesitation, Arthur grabbed her bag and walked back to the car. It was definitely too late to change her mind now. She should have taken the purple shift.

Chapter 17

The house was a spectacular mansion that had been part of Abigail's dowry. Each year, on the December solstice, the ancestral house reopened its doors to host the Yule Ball. The tradition had begun to celebrate Arthur's first birthday, for Abigail had always wanted children and had suffered several miscarriages before giving birth to her son. Even after her death, Robert had insisted on carrying on with the Ball, which by then had become one of the most praised events of the Season, especially if the invitation came with an offer to spend the night at the mansion.

Maya took in the impressive sight the house made under the darkening sky. The multiple windows were framed by exterior illuminations that reflected on the white walls, making them glow. The courtyard was lit by torches and more garlands, the latter installed in the orange trees that had been taken out for the occasion. She couldn't make out the barns and the stables in the backyard but she knew they were somewhere behind the master building; the property was enormous.

Arthur slowed down while driving up the gravelly driveway and stopped at the big front doors. Maya hadn't come to the domain in several years, escaping invitations to the Ball even before her falling out with the Pendletons, and she couldn't help but feel like Cinderella stepping out of her pumpkin when a hired valet opened her door for her.

"Mister Pendleton, your father is already here, as well as several of your guests; please, this way."

She would have found it slightly amusing to have Arthur being shown the way into his own house, if he hadn't placed one arm around her to escort her inside. The hold on her waist was a little hard, although not entirely possessive. He touched her as if he needed to feel something real under his palm. Maya looked up to him, but his face was annoyingly blank, as always; maybe just a little more tense.

Entering the main hall, two familiar figures caught her attention and she escaped Arthur and his moods by running to them.

"Colin! Gavin!"

"Hello Maya. Now, I've got excellent taste, you're gorgeous in this sweater."

His boyfriend slapped Colin's forearm gently and the two exchanged a complicit glance before they sobered themselves as a steward approached Arthur.

"I'm sorry, Sir, I know you requested the Sand Room which is quite spacious, but that's the last one with two beds, and those gentlemen..."

"We'll take another one," Arthur answered sharply.

Her friends looked relieved and though it pained her, Maya understood their uneasiness. High Society was yet to fully admit homosexuality. Hypocrites.

"The Yellow Rose Room is available, Sir. It's smaller but ..."

"Fine."

They climbed up the massive stairs until they reached the first floor and followed their guide to the end of the corridor. The man opened the door and put their luggage inside, before he left with a short bow, closing the door behind them.

The room was not that small, by Maya's standards. The Yellow Rose Room had been named for its windows facing the rose garden in the west wing of the mansion. At sunset, the bright colors reflected on the clear wood panels making them shine. Adding to the impression, the walls were painted a joyous sunny color, which complemented the wood furniture and the deep red curtains.

Maya spun on her heels happily. The room was wonderful. The only problems were the single king size bed, and Arthur.

Suddenly, the mask he held during their arrival began to crack and he looked awfully tired. He walked toward the dresser to fill a glass and drained it in one gulp, refilling it right away.

Maya took it out of his hand to put it away. Arthur growled.

"I'm fine."

"No, you're not."

Maya grabbed him with both hands and led him to a chair.

"Sit. Please."

Obeying seemed the only way for her to let him be, so he did. Talking only added to the pounding in his head. Even keeping his eyes open to watch her whirling around the room was painful. Arthur rested his head on the back of the seat, waiting for the silence to relieve him. The brush on his temples pushed him to open his eyes again and he tried to get away.

"Don't move."

The pressure she applied on his temples momentarily increased the pain and he nearly succumbed to it. Then she began moving her fingers and the circling of her fingertips slowly became comfortable.

Her hands were cool on his feverish skin and his heartbeat calmed down. The gentle touch continued, steadily appeasing the hammering in his head. When the thumping decreased to a more bearable drum, Arthur tried to grab her wrists to make her stop.

"Shush … Let me."

The caress was hypnotic. The movement created a different rhythm in his chest, mysterious and arousing. Arthur inhaled deeply and when Maya removed her hands, he instantly missed the contact.

"Better?"

"Yes; thank you."

The fabric of the covers rustled softly when she sat on the bed.

"Do you have such headaches often?"

"It's nothing."

"I don't believe you; you were as white as a sheet."

The upset in her voice was clear in spite of the hushed tone. Arthur flashed his trademark smirk.

"You sound so worried I might think you like me."

Maya glanced up to the ceiling, sighing, and pushed up on her feet.

"Don't flatter yourself. I need to go home after the ball and I don't feel like taking a taxi for such a ride."

The retort brought another smile, though less arrogant. She moved to her luggage. Arthur gazed at her unpacking for a moment, before he stood up in turn, walking to the window to check on the garden below.

"The migraines come from fatigue and stress. Some people have panic attacks. I have headaches. I stayed up late yesterday to finish with …"

He trailed off, and walked to the bed she had abandoned, testing the firmness of the mattress.

Maya remembered in a rush the heaviness of his hand on her hip earlier; his coming to her apartment the previous Saturday night; and how he had hugged her some days earlier after working all night long. Her heart made a funny little flip at the realization that he seemed to find peace with her.

Feeling a blush creeping up her neck, Maya chose to hide behind a cheeky smile.

"Well, I'll say I'm the best remedy you ever tried."

Arthur laughed and stretched his legs on the bed, settling comfortably on the cushions with his arms folded under his head.

"Who is self-flattering now? We have at least two hours before our presence is required. So if you don't mind, I'll take a nap. Wake me up at six, will you?"

The sweet moment was gone. The young man was back to his obnoxious ways, and apparently, he had decided the bed was his. Maya wondered if she could find Colin and Gavin. If their room had two beds, maybe she could convince them to lend her one for the night.

Arthur called her back at the door.

"Maya, you didn't tell me what color your dress is?"

*

White. She was a dream in white and gold. Arthur lost his footing, half-falling on the bed when he backed up as she walked out of the bathroom. The delicate snowy fabric ran along her curves to attract his eyes to perfect… perfectly inappropriate places. He swallowed more air than saliva and coughed.

Startled by the sound, Maya turned toward him, her eyebrows quirked in an expression of surprise. The small pearls in her hair caught the light and scintillated, as the silken curls flowed freely over one creamy bare attractive shoulder. And her mouth… Her mouth was a brilliant, inviting red. The craving twisting his stomach was unspeakable.

He was probably gawping like a goldfish, for her eyes shone with pleasure. Arthur slowly relaxed his grip on the coverlet, and looked for a compliment. He had to say something, before she realized... For all his eloquence, the only words he found were desperately simple.

"You're beautiful."

"Thanks."

Then she blushed, and a full dictionary invaded his head: beautiful, enchanting, mesmerizing, breathtaking, radiant, ravishing...

The more adjectives he found, the more agitated he felt. Arthur stood and turned his back on her, busying himself with his bow-tie and tux jacket. Surely, in the ballroom with his father and their friends around, he would find his composure. He had to.

Chapter 18

If the peacock attitude was Arthur's way of helping with her growing nerves, it was absolutely… ineffective. Her stomach was so tight its wild looping was reverberating up to her throat.

Maya forced her fingers to unclench from Arthur's sleeve. He looked already too pleased with himself to give him the additional satisfaction of posing as her champion. A part of her wanted to wring his neck. That was the sensible part, he *was* insufferable, treating her like some shiny foil. Another part tried to remind her of the fascination on his face when she stepped out of the bathroom, as if she could find some help in the image. Unfortunately, that part didn't speak loud enough. He didn't seem fascinated now; only vain.

She grasped his forearm again when the ballroom doors opened to let them in. Arthur circled her waist to whisper, steadying her and preventing any possible retreat.

"Quit the rabbit-look, Maya, and smile. My father is watching."

The kiss on her hair felt like a mark. Robert was watching, as well as several guests she didn't recognize. Maya searched frantically for a friendly face; Tristan or Colin, but neither was in her line of sight. Panic chased all coherent thoughts from her head. Robert was watching, and Arthur was guiding (pushing) her straight to him. Her stomach jumped again; her godfather's stare was anything but welcoming.

For an instant, she feared her knees would buckle. Arthur pressed his thumb just below her hip and the intimacy of the touch instantly provoked her. Maya turned to lash out at him, and in doing so she noticed Isobel who was just one step behind

Robert, encouragingly smiling at her. She calmed down; she had no choice, they were already facing her doom.

"Good evening, Father; Regis. Isobel, you're lovely, as usual."

Arthur pecked the offered cheek quickly and was about to present Maya when Robert stepped forward, grabbing her elbow.

"Regis, my ward, Maya Finnegan."

The cold introduction, added to the steel grip, sent goosebumps down her spine. Isobel's father took her hand and kissed her knuckles gallantly.

"My dear, Abigail used to wear white at the Ball, and you're reviving her memory exquisitely."

Robert let go of her and she sensed Arthur stiffened imperceptibly.

'Abigail used to… Oh Lord. And he had said nothing!'

Maya bowed her head silently, desperately wishing for someone to rescue her. Obviously, it would not be her official escort, who was carefully avoiding her eyes.

Salvation came from Isobel, dearest Isobel, who pulled her aside with an admiring squeal.

"Maya, you're stunning! Isn't she stunning? Tristan, tell her she's stunning!"

Her cousin, who had miraculously appeared out of nowhere, took both her hands into his to take a proper look at her and beamed.

"You look absolutely ravishing."

Someone whistled, Tex-Avery wolf style and Colin's laugher echoed behind her:

"Down, Gavin."

The praise from her friends helped her forget the mute disgust in her godfather's icy gaze and Arthur's unnerving demeanor. She accepted a flute of champagne, and the bubbles danced in her empty overturned stomach, making her dizzy. Maya welcomed the feeling, relaxing a little in the smiles and the cheerful company.

"May I?"

The mellow cocoon around her solidified and exploded into pieces when Robert took her wrist to lead her to the dance floor. The orchestra started a famous waltz, and Maya abruptly realized they were to open the ball.

Her stomach back-flipped dangerously. Robert seized her waist before she could find an excuse to flee and started to dance.

They whirled alone to the magical music during a measure or two, before other couples joined them, Isobel and Tristan in the lead. She wanted to watch them dance together, but Robert's massive frame was blocking her view.

"Wearing white doesn't make you the lady of this house. You are my son's guest. Nothing more."

"And nothing less, Father."

The interruption managed to look polite and be a warning at the same time. Her heart fluttered as Arthur replaced his father to carry on with the dance, relieved to be rid of a man who apparently detested her, and exasperated to be so pleased that her savior was his dutiful son.

Maya concentrated on her steps. For once, she was grateful her escort was so tall. Her godfather's disowning had left her too vulnerable to look at Arthur in the eye and keep a straight face. Suddenly, she wanted to cry.

The waltz ended and another one began. Arthur changed his hold on her to bring her closer, her nose nearly brushing his shoulder. Whiffs of musky aftershave grazed her nostrils, and she took in the comforting scent.

"Don't be sad, Edana. You're welcome here; always will be."

Maya looked up and met serious blue eyes.

"Thank you."

The need to be hugged by him tingled on her skin, and she moved back a little, slightly embarrassed. Arthur accepted her retreat with his customary smirk, instantly infuriating her.

"You may want to work on your repartees, though. They're a bit... late; and short."

She would have kicked him if she could have done so without disgracing herself. Left with no other choice, Maya scowled and her companion burst out laughing.

"No pouting; it'll ruin the outfit. Let's go, I'm famished and Colin is probably plundering the buffet already."

The young woman gladly got away from him. Of course Arthur couldn't show consideration or gentleness for more than fifty seconds. She clasped her skirt and pirouetted to join their friends on the other side of the room, perfectly poised. At least this disastrous interlude had settled her nerves completely.

*

The party in full swing was intoxicating. Maya enjoyed dancing with Colin and Gavin, who knew little about ballroom dancing but put so much enthusiasm into their tryouts her head was spinning. Tristan escorted her for most of the complicated quadrilles; they made such a cute couple, even Isobel didn't complain (much).

Arthur waltzed with her a few times, but he spent most of his time fulfilling his duties along his father. However, the more the evening went on, the more he seemed unwilling to leave the happy little group they formed, and whenever he managed to come back, his eyes seemed a little darker each time.

Around midnight, Maya was on a quest for some non-alcoholic beverage to beat the champagne's effects, which were making the floor reel alarmingly, when the tired acceptance reached her ears.

"Yes, of course."

The defeat in Arthur's voice sounded so heartfelt she forgot instantly about her water and walked to the proud figures standing nearby. Robert frowned in response to her brilliant smile while she linked her fingers with Arthur's.

"Dance with me…"

He didn't resist, not even looking back to excuse himself, and she towed him to the dance floor. When he took her in his arms, the gesture held some resemblance of a 'thank you'.

Maybe it was the later hour, maybe it was the champagne, but Maya found his following tease more funny than irritating.

"You missed me."

"Of course not. You always leave too much of an impression for that."

"A compliment, Maya? I'm flattered."

She made a face, the effect spoiled with enough of a smile to make him laugh. Maya's smile widened. She liked his laugh.

"Whatever. I forbid you to talk to your father or his associates for the rest of the night."

"You did miss me. And what did you do to my frightened mouse-like date?"

"I drowned her in golden fizzling bubbles. Can you stop turning so fast?!"

"So you admit I'm turning your head."

Before she could react to the flirting, Arthur suddenly bent her over his forearm in a dip so low her hair brushed the floor.

Maya gave a little cry and when he pulled her up, she clutched to his shoulder, terrified and exhilarated.

"Do that again and you'll sleep on the floor!"

Arthur instantly sobered, eyebrows up; his eyes lit with a mixture of surprise and, which was far more concerning, anticipation.

"You mean I'm not?"

Maya bit her lower lip; she had said that as a joke and hadn't thought he'd take her at her word. She hesitated a little too long and Arthur spoke first, very softly.

"I promise you I..."

"I know."

Maya was glad he pulled her closer so she could hide her flaming face in his chest. And she prayed he upheld whatever promise he had intended to make.

Chapter 19

A silken curl tickled his nose and Arthur instinctively tightened his grip around the warm body curled against him, pulling it closer. His companion sighed softly, and pressed further into him, fast asleep.

He jerked, fully awake, and instantly retrieved the arm that was circling her waist. The movement woke up the raven-haired woman by his side and Maya turned her head to him with a smile.

"Hi... Happy birthday..."

"Huh... Hello. Yeah, thanks."

Maya giggled at the hesitation and grumpy tone. She felt good, rested, and agreeably warm even if he wasn't shielding her from the cold anymore. She stretched luxuriously, delighted to see his dilated eyes trying to focus as far from her as possible. He looked so uncomfortable, she couldn't help teasing him.

"At least you don't snore."

Normally he would have teased back and made some sneaky remark in order to annoy her or make her blush. Blame it on her clear green eyes and mesmerizing smile, Arthur just kept his mouth shut. Maya laughed again and leaned back into the pillows.

"Don't be so cranky. There's nothing wrong with sleeping together. I have shared a bed with Colin and Tristan countless times."

"Colin is gay."

"Tristan is not."

Yeah. And the guy had incredible willpower, or a serious problem, if he had never made a move on her. Arthur couldn't remember the last time he had a woman in his bed, and just slept. It had probably never happened. Or he had been ten at the time. Or sick. Or drunk. No, it had simply never happened.

The shape of Maya next to him was the source of the fever in his veins, propelled by the jumping of his heart. His little traitorous heart, which was probably trying to escape from his chest to reach her.

Temptation was praising her luscious mouth, so close, ready for him to take. His ego insinuated she would not resist if he rolled over her, purring that she might even welcome the assault. Arthur turned his back to her and buried his face in the pillows.

This was just some typical morning reaction; it *had* to be. The craving he had for her was just raging testosterone because her body was too close and half-naked. He didn't want her; he *could not* want her. She was everything he didn't need. She was too candid, too soft-hearted.

So lovely with her hair mussed and that dreamy puff in her eyes... So desirable when she was smiling that impossible smile of hers. He had sworn... Well technically he hadn't promised anything but... He grunted in frustration.

Maya pushed away the covers and got up, apparently perfectly at ease with the situation. He caught a glimpse of her while her night-shift glided down her perfect legs, emerald against ivory. Her silhouette danced in the light when she opened the curtains.

Arthur grunted again. She had no idea how close he was to ravishing her, no idea. He crushed the pillow on his face.

A few minutes later, he realized the room was silent, that she was not moving about anymore. Arthur allowed himself a glimpse above his shield. Maya was settled in an armchair near the window, her knees close to her chest and her arms wrapped around them. She was looking at him with thoughtful eyes.

The green gaze was a little deeper than usual. What had he done to upset her this time? In addition to using her as a pillow half the night and *nearly* harassing her, that was? He took the pillow off his face and pushed up on one elbow. She offered the truth before he had the temerity to ask.

"I don't have a present for your birthday."

One or two possibilities crossed his mind, both of them extremely appealing; and equally inappropriate. Arthur fought to concentrate on something to say without humiliating himself.

"You owe me then."

'Chase your true nature, it comes back in a flash'. How more self-centered could he sound? He wanted to bang his head on the headboard.

His answer seemed to shake her and the cloud shadowing her aquamarine stare dissipated. She really had incredible eyes...

"I guess. I make a sinful chocolate cake if you..."

Was she offering to cook for him? Arthur sat up in the bed.

"I like cake but only if it's shared with friends."

Friendship was good; safe. Friendship lit a spectacular smile on her lips. His mouth dried completely. Friendship was stupid.

"I think it can be arranged... I promised Matthew I'd visit him today. Will you come with me?"

The mention of the child's name finally cut through his disturbing thoughts, until her question sank in.

"No."

The abrupt word immediately dismissed the comfortable atmosphere in the room, chilling the air between them for an excruciating minute. Maya shifted toward the cupboard to pick up her clothes, unwilling to let his attitude spoil her day.

Arthur realized that she had misunderstood his answer.

"I can't. I've got to join my father, we're…" She glanced up at the edge in his voice.

"We're…going to the cemetery."

All of a sudden she remembered that every year Robert insisted that he and Arthur visit Abigail's grave on Arthur's birthday. An unexpected emotion squeezed closed her throat and Maya approached him to put one hand on his arm.

"Do you want me to come with you? I can see Matthew later…"

The spontaneous offer brought a hesitant smile and his eyes cleared to a softer blue. Arthur finally shook his head.

"It's a f…"

He was going to say 'family' and changed his mind. Maya *was* family; at least she used to be. What she was now, he was not ready to name.

"It's a father-son thing. But don't think you're going to escape the baking. I'll pick you up at the hospital afterward to take you home."

The young woman leaned against him to kiss his cheek gently.

"Deal."

The contact lasted a second or two before she moved off the bed, just long enough to tempt him again. Why the heat was suddenly so comforting, he had no clue.

*

Maya hung up the phone and smiled at Isobel.

130

"Sweet as pie... Arthur will come here directly. He said about one hour."

Her friend grinned with mischief.

"And he didn't even complain about the change of plans? Seriously Maya, whatever you're doing to this guy, don't stop on my account..."

Tristan frowned while Maya flushed furiously and busied herself with her food processor. Isobel sat on the counter to watch as she expertly cracked an egg to separate yolk and white. Maya slapped her hand away when she wanted to sample the chocolate chips on display.

"But are you sure you don't want to spend the evening alone? Just the two of you?"

Maya cracked another egg. Tristan cleared his throat and Isobel glowered at him.

"Tristan, how can I get the juicy details if you help her get off the hook?"

"We don't need details. What's between Arthur and Maya is strictly between them."

"You're no fun. Why don't you go set the table or something? So we girls can talk."

She kissed him soundly on the mouth, and shoved him out of the kitchen. Then Isobel turned to Maya, threatening her with a rubber spatula.

"Now, I *want* details. It's not like Arthur to spend a Saturday night at home over home-made dinner, especially on his birthday."

"Nothing's wrong with that."

Maya added sugar to her mixture and hid behind the buzz from the processor. Isobel handed her the next ingredients but refused to recoil.

"Oh come on, Maya. There's something cooking between you two and I'm not talking about birthday cake."

The raven-haired woman checked the oven before she added flour, butter and cocoa to the mix and pretended to focus on her recipe. Two minutes later, she was done, and put the mixture to bake. Isobel picked up the dirty bowls to wash them, while her friend started on the frosting.

"There's nothing to tell, really. We... We're just... We're trying to figure each other out, I think. This thing between us, it's...unexpected."

Maya paused. It was hard to explain without telling the *entire* truth. She wanted to tell Isobel and ask for advice but she had promised. Her next words came out even more softly.

"I don't know what to make of him. One minute he is irksome and obnoxious and a complete jerk and the next he's so..."

"Lovable?" Isobel offered.

"Talking about me?"

Colin entered the kitchen with a broad grin and an enormous plate in his arms.

"My famous spinach and ricotta chicken breasts..."

Maya kissed his cheek and took the plate off his hands.

"Of course we're talking about you. Who else?"

He mimicked profound brainwork.

"Hum... You forgot to mention irresistibly funny, handsome and brilliant, so it could have been my other half."

"The better half, you mean."

Gavin picked up the spoon to sample Maya's chocolate mix. Isobel laughed.

"Sorry guys. Party boy was the topic."

Colin sighed heavily and hid his face in his boyfriend's shoulder to fake a sob. Gavin patted his head and winked at Maya.

"So, what is it exactly between you and Arthur?"

The young woman felt her cheeks go pink again. Where did they miss their part that their friends doubted the pairing?

Or did Gavin know? Colin had surely promised Arthur not to tell anything to anyone but had he extended that to his boyfriend? If Gavin knew, why was he asking?

The oven beeped to signal it was halfway through the cooking-time and Maya used the distraction to evade the probing. She couldn't explain more than what she already had confessed to Isobel. Arthur unsettled her. She never knew if he would act like an idiot or show he cared.

Because he did care under that mask of indifference he wore all the time. He cared about Matthew and about being honourable. He cared about living up to his father's expectations. He concealed his heart to survive the impossible pressure of being the Heir of the Pendleton Empire, and it seemed to be eating him alive.

Suddenly, Maya wanted Arthur to be there, so she could close her arms around him and create a shelter for him to rest. The fact she enjoyed holding him would only add to the comfort. It couldn't be a bad thing…

"By the way, Maya, I think an alien abducted half of your tree."

Gavin's remark pulled her out of her reverie. Tristan, who had followed, answered for her.

"No such luck. She did that on purpose."

His cousin squared her shoulders and prepared for another battle about the rights of Christmas trees but the doorbell cut through her growing indignation. Isobel pushed her out of the kitchen.

"Here comes Prince Charming. Hurry up before he turns back into a frog."

Chapter 20

Thanks to all their questions, Maya felt completely helpless in front of Arthur. He didn't seem totally at ease either when he put one arm around her to hug her quickly.

His heartbeat was hurried under her hand and she refused to let him step away, holding him just a moment longer. Arthur brushed a kiss on her forehead and whispered,

"I'm fine."

She didn't believe him. He was keeping her close and played his role even if they were alone in the room. He was far from fine. And he was so sure she was going to accept his bravado without asking and just walk away from him...

The idea he misjudged her displeased Maya and she frowned. Maybe Arthur sensed the annoyed pout against his shoulder, because she felt the grin that always preceded the banter growing in her hair.

"I saw Colin's car outside. I hope you made two cakes..."

"The cake... The cake! Oh God!!"

She forgot instantly about Arthur and rushed to the kitchen. Left alone, Arthur stepped further into her living-room, leaving his coat on the back of the couch.

Someone had lit the tree. All the decorations made it look all the more quirky. You had to be Maya to resist the urge to chop it down. Only she could see more than there was in her pitiful tree. Or would offer comfort because she cared enough to know it was needed, even if she had no obligation to do so.

Arthur shook his head, dismissing the thought. He couldn't allow her to fall for him. He couldn't afford to care himself. With care came love, and love complicated things. It brought confusion and failure. Loss.

"Oh, no you don't."

The severe tone of Tristan stopped his gesture toward his coat.

"Maya went to a lot of trouble so you can celebrate your birthday like a normal person for once. So you will stay exactly where you are."

Arthur sneered.

"The exact spot?"

"Don't play that game with me."

The door opened and Isobel entered the soon-to-be battlefield with some things to put on the table. She instantly detected the tension between the two men and came near Tristan, circling his waist.

The young man linked his fingers with hers, bringing her hand to his lips to kiss it lightly.

"Give us a minute Isobel, please."

The blonde nodded and returned to the joyous chorus formed by Colin and Gavin's laughter. The cheerful atmosphere of the kitchen starkly contrasted with the glacial living-room. Maya noticed at once the look on her friend's face.

"What's the matter?"

She took one step toward the door but Isobel stopped her.

"Don't. They need to clear things up by themselves."

Maya agreed silently and returned to her salad, not completely at ease leaving Arthur and Tristan alone if they were on the verge of fighting. She was not sure who she pitied the most either.

Despite the coming argument, Arthur grinned.

"I must say you're the first person I've seen her yield to."

Tristan kept a straight face, but his opponent caught a flash of amusement (or male pride) in the dark stare. Arthur glanced toward the kitchen. Explanations or threats had to be quick. He settled for the truth.

"I don't want to hurt her."

"Then it is better you stop this masquerade now."

"I can't; not yet."

"Why not?"

The question echoed in the room. Why not stop pretending they were an item? Isobel had obviously no intention of joining in their fathers' plot, even less now that Tristan had entered the scene. It would probably take weeks or even months before Robert would come up with another suitable candidate.

Arthur snorted. He could walk away now, and spare himself the constant torture. He could deal with Matthew's case from afar. Except (he didn't want to) there was this other little problem…

"My father wants to close the Foundation. As long as he believes Maya and I are an item, he will let me handle the case."

That was all Arthur could safely disclose. However, Tristan filled in the blanks bitterly.

"Because she is a member of the board and you can use her to access information privy only to us."

Arthur chose to leave the barely concealed accusation unanswered, not even nodding.

"Are you? Are you going to use her like that?"

The outraged question maddened him instantly.

"Of course not! What do you take me for?!"

Tristan sat on the couch with such a defeated air shadowing his features the tension between them decreased at once. Arthur narrowed his eyes. He was a member of the board and Maya's cousin and maybe he was just as innocent...

"So it's true."

Arthur let him go on without interrupting.

"When we discovered P and A had had the account blocked, I tried to obtain some answers. But Moira... Let's say she is less than cooperative."

His instinct was telling him Tristan was sincere. Arthur stayed quiet.

"I asked the bank to provide me with the details of our financial operations."

This time, the blond man reacted.

"Whatever is in those documents is very dangerous, Tristan, and I'm not talking about my father or Moira. I can help, but you have to trust me."

He was asking a lot and he knew it. Arthur just hoped Tristan was sufficiently intelligent to put aside their differences and believe him. He wanted to help. He wanted to do the right thing. He wanted to clear the Foundation of the bastards who had hijacked it so the account could be unfrozen. Then Maya would be able to help more children like Matthew. And she would be happy.

"Do you know what's wrong with Moira?"

The question broke Arthur's train of thought.

"We have suspicions. But I don't have any proof."

The other man considered the evasive answer for an instant.

"I need to think about it. We'll talk again."

This was as close to an agreement as they could reach. A giggle came from behind the kitchen door. Tristan stood.

"They're having fun over there. How about we join them?"

Maya watched her cousin's face attentively when they entered but Isobel distracted him and he turned away. Arthur was also unreadable; she let him greet Colin and Gavin before approaching him.

"Is everything okay?"

"Sure."

He put one arm over her shoulders, dragging her closer until their hips bumped.

"With a cousin like him, you don't need a brother to warn your boyfriend to treat you like a queen."

Maya laughed and escaped his touch.

"You'd better listen then. Dinner's ready everyone!"

*

Arthur handed her the last dried glass to store and leaned with his back against the counter. The cozy situation set all his alarm bells ringing; wiping the dishes after dinner with friends had the exact glint of… He refused to label it commitment. Commitment meant obligation; compromise.

This didn't apply to what he shared with Maya. What he had with her was a deal. They had a deal to save a life and help him out of his father's grasp. Nothing more.

She took the drying cloth from his hand to fold it over the oven knob expertly. When she looked around to make sure all was in place, her hair danced around her face. She was lovely.

Satisfied with her examination, Maya started toward the living room before she noticed Arthur hadn't moved.

"Are you coming?"

"Yeah, yeah sure. It's late anyway, you're probably tired. I'll go."

Maya glanced at the clock, then back at him. It was barely ten-thirty. She switched off the lights in the kitchen and Arthur had no choice but to follow. She nestled on the couch comfortably, her legs under her.

The soft glow of the lamps on her cheek was distracting.

"What did you and Tristan talk about earlier?"

The chair facing her seemed safer. Arthur sat on its arm, ready to flee at the first sign of too much contentment.

"I told you; just cousin to boyfriend's warning."

"Arthur, Tristan knows this is just a set-up. You're not my boyfriend."

"How come you don't have one?"

He hadn't intended to ask that. He just wanted to divert the conversation. She was refusing his explanation of Tristan's admonishing him to keep his hands off her. He wanted to know. Why was she single? Maya was beautiful, brilliant, caring... What sort of idiots did she date who let her escape?

He hated himself for asking when sadness surfaced in her voice.

"Men are not interested in me."

"Ridiculous."

She lifted curious eyes (too clear, too bright) to him and Arthur shifted on his seat uncomfortably. Maya focused on her remote control again.

"Will you stay for a movie?"

It was easy to picture himself settled on the couch with her watching some grade-Z movie. Somewhere in the middle of the flick, she would snuggle against him and fall asleep. He would carry her to bed and she would not let go of him so he would lie down with her. And maybe in the morning, she would decide she wanted more than chaste kisses and false caresses. Arthur pushed onto his feet.

"Maybe some other time, Edana. Sweet dreams."

He kissed her forehead and took his leave.

Maya grabbed a cushion and curled up on the couch, going through the programs on TV, uninterested. She couldn't force him to stay if he didn't want to. The apartment seemed empty without him. She would have liked it if he had stayed and watched TV with her; she would probably have leaned on him at some point, and fallen asleep surrounded by his warmth. And maybe he would have stayed the night and she would have woken up with him in the morning...

All the movies were Christmas cheesy romances she knew by heart. Maya switched off the TV.

SECOND CHANCES

Chapter 21

Going shopping on a Sunday afternoon two days before Christmas was the craziest idea she had ever had, Maya decided.

The bus was crowded; the sidewalks were slippery with slush; and customers had apparently left their 'goodwill' spirit at home. A bony woman with an acid-green hat hit her in the chest with an umbrella, and when Maya squealed in pain, the woman only glared and haughtily proceeded to the door.

The young woman had had enough. She paid for the cookbook she intended to give Colin and Gavin and exited the store. Reaching the central coffee shop, she ordered some hot chocolate and reviewed her list. She had Tristan's music papers and some earrings for Isobel. She had bought Moira's and Cedric's presents at the Market the previous week.

The only ones left were Matthew's and Arthur's. Both were a problem, thought a different one. She had tons of ideas for Matthew's present: pyjamas, books, collector cards, toys, and could not settle on only one thing. As for Arthur...

The truth was for Arthur she had no clue. Nothing. Zilch. Zero. Nada.

Her beverage arrived and she turned to check the store map in case an idea struck. She categorically refused a gift-card; it was too impersonal. A tie was also out of the question... even if she could just see his face if she presented him with the one with little Snoopy, which she had spotted earlier. Priceless.

He didn't read or favor one particular kind of music, so books and CDs were not an option. The chocolate was deliciously creamy. Maya sampled more and continued with the list of stores: no DVDs (did he even own one?), no jewelry, no gadget for sushi-making; he apparently liked sushi, but she was allergic to seafood so it was not an option either. Though her allergies had nothing to do with it, of course; she simply didn't feel he would like home devices. Aftershave was interesting but so easy... and she liked his, anyway. Thus to change it was absurd.

Maya was nearly at the end of the list, and still completely uninspired. One store specialized in sweaters for men. She could buy him a pullover. She knew he liked blue and basic colors, and she had a pretty good idea of his size... Go for a sweater.

She wrapped her fingers around the cup. A pullover was completely boring. A piece of clothing could be interpreted as intimate and territorial. She could not buy him that.

Maya sighed. Matthew was easier, she was going for Matthew's present first and prayed a merciful muse would attack her in the meantime.

The toy store was so full Maya nearly gave up and turned tail without even entering. Only the anticipation of the child's pleasure when opening his present pushed her forward.

Thankfully, only the cashiers were overloaded (which promised hours of waiting for later) and the aisles were (relatively) accessible. Inside, the clerks were disguised as elves and answered parents while the children ran all around the place. The kids had so many stars in their eyes her spirit lifted instantly. She had the impression of having entered Mr. Magorium's Wonder Emporium, just waiting for a cube to fly by her.

Maya reached the aisle she was looking for and began inspecting the stuffed animal-shaped slippers on display. The horses looked a bit like cows, and she frowned, unconvinced.

"Can I help you? How old is your little one?"

"Eight years old. But he is not…"

"I suggest you get a nine-year-old size. They grow up quick at this age."

The elf pressed a pair in her hands with an encouraging smile. A little girl behind Maya started crying, to the despair of an already stressed mom. The clerk excused herself and went to offer help with the capricious girl. Maya looked down at the horse-cow-like pair of slippers in her hand, and at the teary girl and her heart sank.

Matthew was eight years old and she had no idea if he'd ever be nine. He was a loving kid, without a mother to sing a lullaby to him or make him cookies for school. He didn't have a father to play with or read him a story. Suddenly, the pouting of the girl seemed unbearable. The heaviness in her chest was so painful.

A ring stopped the upcoming tears, but her voice choked a bit when she answered her cell phone.

'Hi. Are you at the hospital? I hear crying.'

"No, I'm shopping for Christmas presents."

'You don't sound like your usual self. Are you all right?'

The question surprised her a little. Then she remembered that behind the cold mask, Arthur had a heart, a golden heart if one could come by it. The tightness in her throat eased a little.

"And how do I usually sound?"

'With me? Annoyed and bossy. Will you buy me a present?'

Maya nearly laughed. She could picture him behind his desk, with that cocky grin he had when he teased her and his eyes a soft blue.

"Do you deserve one?"

'Probably not.'

The banter disintegrated the earlier spell completely and she grinned frankly.

"I'll see what I can do then. Did you have a reason for calling?"

'Yes. I was wondering...'

The hesitation sobered her instantly; she felt uneasy when her heart fluttered. Arthur was nothing more than her fake boyfriend. He... No. *She* didn't want anything else.

'What are we going to do for Christmas Eve? I am to have dinner with my father, and you with your family... We can hardly put my father and Moira in the same room.'

"Unless you're up for remodelling afterward. Not to mention the thermo-nuclear overcooking for the turkey, of course."

Arthur laughed out loud and the sound jingled joyfully in her ear. Then he became serious again. She cupped the phone, as if it could bring him closer.

He cleared his throat. It was strange to refer to them as a 'we'; they were talking about keeping up the pretence, only making sure their arrangement stayed a secret; yet the pronoun came up naturally. The images crossing his mind were absurd, the two of them at her place or his, sharing dinner and enjoying each other's... company. Enjoying each other's company. He pushed the ludicrous fantasies away and sealed his fate.

"I will call you during the evening, so it'll look like I miss you, and we'll see each other at the Christmas Tree event."

She kept silent on the other side of the line; Arthur realized how hard and cold the statement was. The idea her eyes were flooding with tears was unbearable. His grasp on the phone tightened.

"Maya?"

'Yes, yes that's fine. I think I will buy Matthew horse-shaped slippers.'

Her voice almost sounded normal. He had hurt her. His conversation with Tristan the previous evening rushed back to his mind. He could only hurt her. Arthur accepted the change of subject, downcast.

"I bought him a helmet for his riding lessons."

'You did?'

The genuine pleasure in her question wiped out whatever was weighing on his stomach. Arthur beamed and found he was unable to erase the smile from his face. He had to stop that now.

"He'll need it. I'll call you on Tuesday night."

'Okay. Would you...'

He didn't wait for the rest of her question and hung up. Emotions were surfacing too easily: feelings he was not supposed to have and should not encourage.

Maya looked at her phone, her eyes narrowing in surprise, and hurt giving way to annoyance. Arthur could really act like a jerk. This side of him she was definitely *not* attracted to.

SECOND CHANCES

Chapter 22

The waiter walked away with their empty plates and Arthur looked around. As usual, Robert had chosen to have their Christmas Eve dinner in one of the fanciest restaurants in town. The atmosphere was quiet and the food, of course, delicious. However, it was the last way Arthur would have chosen to celebrate if he'd had a choice. Flashes of messy tables and his mother's patient demeanor with his childhood exuberance haunted him briefly.

The memories were bittersweet and scattered, so Arthur dismissed them shifting in his chair to settle more comfortably, while his father went on about his current obsession, the Mercia negotiations.

The phone carefully stored in his jacket bumped against his side when he moved. Arthur slipped his hand into his pocket to touch it and his father's voice faded once more. The contact awoke anticipation, tainted with guilt. He ended his conversation with Maya without a goodbye and didn't call back. She was probably going to lash him when he interrupted her own party. Maybe she would not even answer the call, making him sweat for his bad behavior.

Or maybe she would simply throw a dagger or two so he felt bad, before stating he was lucky it was Christmas. And the truth would be she already knew he hated himself and her generous heart had already forgiven him. His thumb played along the plastic case, caressing the screen slowly.

She was probably laughing, her vivid eyes sparkling with pleasure as she played house and helped everybody with food or drinks, just as she had the previous Saturday. He should have called earlier. On Sunday, when he wanted to apologize; on

Monday when he was already dying to do so. Earlier today, when he wanted to tell her… to offer wishes for the coming celebration. If he called now, he would disturb her and by the time he went home, it would be too late.

"… I'm flying to Mercia on Thursday morning, so I need you to revise the contract tom…"

"I'm sorry father, I'm busy tomorrow."

Robert narrowed glacial gray eyes on his son and they entered another glare contest. Those were becoming more and more frequent, Arthur realized, but his 'seeing' Maya had only enhanced the process. It'd been a while since he refused to blindly obey his father's orders; until Maya, the resistance had been more passive. Like keeping his mother's coat of arms on his official communication, or doing things his own way despite Robert's instructions.

"Are you jeopardizing our work for a woman, Arthur? I do hope you have more sense than that."

"I am not risking anything, Father. Your experience will more than compensate for the revision, and given that our client is as crafty as you are, I don't doubt I'll have some more to do anyway. What's the point in doing things twice? You taught me better than wasting time and effort for nothing."

The sharp intake of air from his father told Arthur he had hit a nerve. Robert could not retort without going against his own lectures. However, hoping the hard man would settle at that was wishful thinking.

"So I thought. But given you're still pursuing some idle girl, I'm not so sure you have learned that lesson."

The insult sank in and his hand fisted around the phone. Somehow, Arthur managed to keep his voice low, and relatively calm.

SECOND CHANCES

"I would greatly appreciate it if you'd stop disregarding Maya. She makes me happier than I've been in years; if that in itself is not enough, do remember she is your ward and that you once considered her as a daughter. Please excuse me."

He felt so angry his legs wobbled when he pushed up on his feet; Arthur straightened up proudly, unwilling to show how much the argument weakened him and he walked to the lodge.

The young man gestured to the barman for a double bourbon. When he forgot for a moment he couldn't have her and let her aura surround him, Maya did make him happy; peaceful. Maybe when this whole affair ended, if she didn't hate him, they would find their way into some neutral territory and try to understand each other.

Arthur took the phone out of his pocket to put it near the glass in front of him. The alcohol warmed his stomach, helping him to regain some of his composure. He had no desire to worry her, as she surely would if he didn't wait a little to call. Whatever happened in the future, he would not tolerate his father hurting her further. It hurt him as well.

*

The ring made Maya jump. Tristan got up with an apologetic smile, quickly erased by a brilliant beam when he read the name on the screen. The young man greeted Isobel and moved away for some privacy.

Maya grinned and winked at her sister, despite the sting Arthur's silence created. In spite of his abrupt hanging-up two days earlier, she was sure he would keep his word and call. But he had still to do so.

One hand ventured low in her back and she glared at the man on her left. Cedric laughed, completely unashamed.

151

"Kitty Cat, you look ravishing tonight."

"Thank you. Who wants more pie?"

Having no answer, she stood to clear the table. Moira's fiancé laughed even more loudly, and squeezed her sister's knee, letting his hand move up her thigh a lot more than etiquette usually tolerated. Moira returned his lazy sneer, to Maya's growing displeasure.

Since the man was back in town, her sister was once again calm and smiling, clearly high on cloud 9. Moira didn't even care her beau made passes at her baby sister and Maya wished she had an excuse to ask Tristan to drive her home. If Mighty Arthur could grant her a call…

Salvation came from her cousin, who returned with some good news.

"Isobel will fly back tomorrow morning; her parents are going to the Riviera for New Year's Eve but she prefers to come here. Her flight is rather early so Maya, if you don't mind, we'll give the love-birds some privacy."

God she loved that man. Arthur had a couple of lessons to learn, but Cedric could sign up for a full-time class and still need more. Pig.

Tristan left after one hot chocolate and several teases about Isobel ('I told you you'd like her' / 'shut up, Maya') with the promise to meet before the frenzy began at the Vallon Hospital to help with last-minute details for the event. She noticed her voicemail was blinking when she turned from the door and pressed the 'play' button.

'Hi Maya, Arthur speaking. I… I wanted to… I wish you a Merry Christmas.'

Perplexed, she played the message again. They were supposed to make it look like they missed each other, so why on Earth had he called home instead of her cell? She checked it for missed calls for the hundredth time and, of course, found none, like the ninety-nine first times... Was there a problem?

Maya anxiously dialed Arthur's number, uncaring about the late hour.

'Hello?'

His reply sounded sleepy.

"Arthur? I just got your message..."

The allusion flew in the wind, probably because he was yawning. She looked for something to say, feeling ridiculous. Even half-asleep, he was faster.

'Did you have nice evening?'

"Yes, thank you. We were at Moira's and Cedric's. Tristan drove me back just a little while ago. Isobel is coming back tomorrow. What about you?"

'Dinner at the Castle Tower. Food was great. Company needs improvement.'

She heard the ruffle of sheets, as he certainly backed against his pillows. Maya chastised herself as soon as her mind wondered if he wore a shirt. He hadn't the previous weekend.

"I should let you go back to sleep. Thanks for calling, and merr–"

'Wait!'

Arthur sounded fully awake now. Her heartbeat started to race, skipping a beat or two in the way, only to slow down again when he asked, *'What time do I pick you up tomorrow morning? Is nine all right?'*

She forced a smile into her voice.

"If you make that eight thirty, I'll offer coffee."

'Lady, add pancakes to that and I'll be there at seven.'

Maya giggled.

"Are you bargaining again?"

SECOND CHANCES

'I never bargain about pancakes. Eight o'clock, toasts and coffee. That's my last offer.'

"Eight it is, then... Good night, Arthur; merry Christmas."

'Merry Christmas Maya.'

Chapter 23

The pen scratched the paper clasped on the clip-board and Maya looked at the following item on her list: buffet arrangements. The caterer was already busy around the tables so she marked this one off as well.

A giggle forced her to look up and she caught sight of Isobel who was pulling Tristan under another garland. They were supposed to verify if the list of received presents matched the attendants' one. Apparently, testing the mistletoe was far more interesting.

She grabbed the forgotten lists before she approached the giant tree on the opposite side of the room and the man in front of it. Arthur didn't move when she stopped by his side. Maya glanced at him quickly then at the tree he was watching.

"They are beautiful, aren't they? Each child made a card to decorate the tree."

Arthur tore his gaze away from the Christmas cards hung in the branches to look at her. She smiled gently and he looked away. She liked the way light was playing on his hair to make it shine like gold. His blue eyes were always so serious, except when he seemed to forget himself and tease her. The way his casual sports-wear flattered his figure didn't hurt the eye either. He was a handsome man. He looked... hot.

Maya felt warmth coming up her throat; some days, she really hated her skin, which revealed all her emotions. Arthur didn't notice or pretended not to.

"Do you need some help?"

Tristan and Isobel were experiencing another mistletoe bunch. An itch of envy bothered her for a second, quickly dismissed. Her cousin and his new flame created a whirlwind of happiness around them and Maya was glad they had found each other (with a little help from her…). She stared at her so-called boyfriend and winked.

"The other elves are busy… Do you mind comparing the lists?"

Arthur nodded in agreement and returned his attention to the tree. Maya slipped one hand around his elbow to tug him toward a nearby table.

He thought about resisting. He was stronger and she would certainly lose her balance if he stood his ground. Catching her if she did was more than tempting. She had been torturing him since he reached her door with fresh pastries at eight o'clock, maybe on purpose, most probably not. Her dazzling smiles and inviting glances were stealing his breath away every time.

Maya felt his hesitation and turned her head toward him.

One long strand of hair escaped her hairclip and his gaze followed the wild curl down her shoulder, brushing her bosom to fall on their now-linked fingers. She smiled and Arthur wondered why he had not yet pulled her under one of those garlands to kiss her senseless. She would not deny him. He knew she wouldn't. It was not his ego speaking. Her touch, her smile echoed deep inside him to tell him she was happy to be here with him.

Arthur stared at their entwined hands, unable to break free just yet, and cleared his throat.

"Is coffee coming along with the burden?"

Maya took the repartee for what it was, a way to escape the troubling intimacy that was growing between them, going far beyond their pretending. She laughed and reached up to kiss his cheek, just because she wanted to, indulging in the caress, secretly thrilled when she felt him tense in return.

"I have to see Moira about the payment for the caterer and the entertainment. I'll stop by the cafeteria on my way back."

"Black, no sugar."

"I know that."

Her grin was addictive. Arthur stepped back to pick up her clipboard and scanned the lists while she walked out of the room. The smile on his lips felt nearly as good as her kiss.

*

Maya paused at the half-opened door. Moira had her back to her and was fumbling with her purse. Cedric was nowhere to be seen, which suited her just fine.

The young woman rapped on the frame and entered the office. At the noise, Moira turned briskly, beaming, but her hopeful welcome faded when she recognized her baby-sister.

"Oh, it's you…"

"Hi Moira."

Maya ignored the pang of pain from the gloomy greeting and smiled.

"Are you looking for something?"

Her sister quickly unclenched her fingers from her purse, pushing it away nervously.

"No. What are you doing here?"

The snap shocked Maya and she replied without thinking.

"I'm very happy to see you too, Moira. If I need help? Oh, no, thank you, fortunately Arthur, Tristan and Isobel are giving me a hand. It's so kind of you to ask."

The blonde woman frowned.

"There is no need to be harsh."

"You had no need to bite my head off, either."

Moira softened and came to slide one arm around her baby-sister's shoulders.

"I'm sorry, I've got a headache. Too much drinking yesterday with too little sleep. Can I help you with something?"

Her explanation instantly deflated Maya, who enfolded her arms around her in turn.

"Do you want aspirin, or…"

"Now this is a fantasy come true."

The sneer in Cedric's voice made Maya tense at once. Moira abruptly moved from her embrace to grab his arm.

"Do you have them? Please…"

The distasteful man fished an envelope from his breast pocket, but kept it out of Moira's anxious reach.

"Calm down, Moira, you're worrying your mouth-watering little sister."

"She is not well, Cedric, now is not the time for your stupid games."

Her sister hungrily opened the seal and swallowed a pink pill; Maya bit back the other epithets, uneasy. She had seen people in pain craving relievers such morphine, opium, or other addictive substances, but Moira claimed she simply had a migraine. Aspirin wasn't… Moira was readying to pick another one when her fiancé stopped her.

"Only one, Moira, those are powerful. Wait for its effects."

Her sister was leaning against her desk, eyes closed. Her face was slowly relaxing as the medicine acted. Maya took one step forward.

"Can I see these?"

Cedric pocketed the envelope again and approached her.

"Maybe… If you ask very nicely."

How dare he be so sleazy with his fiancée in the room! Maya stepped back but he blocked her retreat, his lustful eyes running along her body. She swallowed hard, suddenly dreading how far he would go. And Moira apparently didn't care! Her sister had reopened her eyes and fixed an amused glaze on them. Maya squealed when Cedric played with her hair.

She slapped his hand away and tried to pass by him toward the door.

"Now now, don't be such a prude. You don't wear that kind of skirt to have men behave around you…"

A decided punch on the door gave her the diversion she needed to escape. Arthur entered the room without waiting. He took in her distress immediately and moved forward, shielding her from the couple's view. Moira hissed between her teeth as Cedric cast suspicious glances from him to Maya. Arthur ignored them and turned to the gentle woman standing so close he could feel her anxiety bouncing against him.

"The caterer asked for his payment."

She nodded but made no move toward the desk and her sister. The blonde growled.

"Send him here. I'll take care of it."

Maya was all too happy to take her word for it and she grabbed her champion's arm in a discreet beg for him to escort her out of the office.

Arthur led her to the cafeteria, ordering coffee. She appreciated the thoughtful gesture, which bought her time to regroup before facing their friends again. They sat in a corner, sipping their beverage in silence for a while, before she asked, "Do you think my skirt is too short?"

The question astonished him for a second, before he let his gaze rest on the green velvet that stopped a couple of inches above her knees, to bare her long legs. He'd never been such a goner for legs. But hers were really… Were very…

"I like it just fine."

His grin was just one shade above wolfish. Maya flushed and chuckled.

"You're silly…"

Silly or not, her blush calmed down the angry beast who wanted to rip apart the brute who had harassed her. Arthur didn't want her wonderful face to be shadowed again so he changed the subject to one he was sure would please her.

"I thought we could go and fetch Matthew now."

Maya beamed, and pushed on her feet.

"Yes!"

Arthur drained the rest of his coffee and offered his hand. The lion inside his chest started to purr when she took it.

Chapter 24

Isobel tugged at Tristan's sleeve to get his attention and the young man instantly turned away from Gavin to circle her waist and pull her closer. She laughed and allowed him one kiss before putting a finger on his chin to force him to look to his right.

"Aren't they adorable?"

She was referring to the trio formed by Matthew, Arthur and Maya. All were seated on the floor near the tree. The kid was jittering his feet like mad, laughing his head off because Arthur was tickling him through his brand-new slippers. And Maya was trying to calm him down long enough to take the black helmet off his head.

She said something, visibly ordering Arthur to stop, which resulted in Matthew attacking her legs. Tristan glared, as Arthur immobilized Maya without hesitation so the child won the advantage in their battle.

"We should…"

"Absolutely not."

Isobel grabbed her boyfriend's hand, forbidding him to fly to his cousin's rescue. They watched until Matthew's interest in their game faded, his attention switched to the magician who had taken the stage with a white rabbit. Isobel had a satisfied glint in her gray eyes and Tristan an expression that was all but appreciative.

Arthur released his grasp slowly and stretched to recover a package from under the tree.

"Merry Christmas."

Maya looked at the package on her lap then to him, her eyes widened in surprise and childish pleasure. After ogling it from all sides, she finally decided to pull on the tape, slowly unwrapping her present. She was so cautious Arthur nearly took it out of her hands to finish exposing the objects inside for her.

"Oh!"

The small clay figurines in the carved box were delicately painted. The magi wore bright colored cloaks, crimson red, deep green, and sunny yellow. One of the shepherds had a lamb on his shoulders. Another one held a stick. She carefully unwrapped two more sheep, and a camel. The box also contained empty shells for the characters of the nativity set she already possessed and for future purchases.

Maya put her presents back into their box before she leaned toward Arthur to brush his cheek lightly, and suddenly he couldn't move. His arms stayed useless by his side while her lips curved into another of her mysterious smiles.

"Thank you."

It took him a few seconds to collect one neuron or two to croak a "You're welcome."

Still grinning, Maya pushed one little package into his hand.

"Open mine."

Frozen, Arthur looked at the homemade wrapping. Maya's package had a big silver bow, clearly scissors-curled on the ends. His father generally stuck to gift cards or checks in a thick vellum envelope; other presents he received were professionally handled by shop clerks. He couldn't remember the last time someone had taken the time to choose something for him and wrap it. There were little penguins dancing all over the paper. It looked completely ridiculous and it was perfect.

She blushed, vaguely unnerved by his concentrated stare.

"It's not much. I…"

"I'm sure it's great."

He tore the wrapping feverishly and burst out laughing. She had picked three toy cars, a blue police car, a firefighter truck, and a yellow race-car he recognized to be a transformer.

"It was Mark's idea. He said you have to have your own, because he is out of the hospital and if you want to play…"

She shut up, annoyed with her babbling. Why was she so nervous? It was just a silly present to keep up the pretence. Uncomfortable, she shifted and her knee brushed the wood box by her side. Suddenly she remembered the Christmas Market some days earlier.

She hadn't found her magi there and had been disappointed. Arthur had taken the time to choose something personal and thoughtful, and she had grabbed some stupid toys. She would pay him back for the sculptures and–

"This is the best present I've had in years, Edana."

Arthur was smiling, and she didn't know what to make of the glint in his blue eyes, so she circled his neck, and pressed her mouth to his.

Her kiss took him off guard and God… he was only human; he gave into it without a second thought. She was soft and sweet. Her lips tasted of the icing from the cupcake she had eaten, and coffee. She was delicious. Arthur fought to quiet the need growing inside him and keep their embrace chaste, yet his control began to escape him when she abandoned herself against his chest, all pretence gone. He freed her abruptly, short of breath, desperately looking for annoyance in her misty eyes to steady himself.

Maya couldn't wrap her head around anything but Arthur. This kiss, their first real kiss, was one he intended to give or one she wanted to take or the other way around, she wasn't sure.

It lasted only a few seconds, but when he pushed her away she could barely remember why there were so many people around them. She wanted to lean forward to kiss him again, but his hands on her shoulders stopped her. He looked sad and it confused her even more.

"Thank you."

She couldn't tell if Arthur was thanking her for his present, or for the kiss. Maybe both.

*

"What the hell, Arthur!"

Tristan slammed the door behind him. Arthur kept washing his hands. The water was icy cold but he didn't give a damn. Tristan narrowed his eyes on the man who had his back to him. The silent attitude was so far from the arrogance Arthur usually presented he hesitated. He might not have his cousin's gift for empathy, but he could recognize pain when he saw it.

They looked at each other in the mirror.

"What I do, what I have to do" Arthur automatically corrected "is going to hurt her. *I* will hurt her. But God help me, I can't stay away… It will end badly but I just can't. I…"

'I love her.'

The idea lingered there, surprising and warm. What he felt was not infatuation, or a simple crush. It was past lust, though desire was there, of course. It was more than that. Her smile was the ultimate prize to win and he could not stand to imagine her tears. He loved her. He would give her the world, the moon, the stars or let her go just as well, if she wanted to.

He loved her and he couldn't have her; like all he held dear in the past, he would lose her; she would disappear, leave him alone and heartbroken. He loved her and it wasn't enough. The hole inside him when he considered the future was white hot and icy cold, so dark he wanted to scream and so empty he felt like a part of him was dying.

Arthur leaned against the sink, not caring about the water that was still running. Tristan took one step closer, and landed one hand on his shoulder. Arthur was annoying, and conceited, but instinct told him he was a good man, nonetheless. Maybe what he needed in order to fully accept himself was Maya, and her capacity to love without reserve.

"You should give yourself a little credit. Maybe…"

Arthur squared his shoulders and shook off the other man's hand.

"I have to go. Tell her my father called or something."

"I won't lie for you. And you'll tell her everything yourself, but not today. Walk back in there and be your usual charming self. It's Christmas, after all."

Arthur bowed his head in silence. He knew better than to hope Maya would forgive him when she learned the role he had in the Foundation's inquiry. To ignore that for a few hours would only make it harder later. He just couldn't help craving for one last bit of happiness.

*

Exhausted, Matthew fell asleep sometime during the puppet show. Maya brushed Arthur's arm, pointing at the child and he moved forward to scoop him up, while she collected his things.

The corridors were peaceful while they walked back to Matthew's room, side by side. The little boy's head had come to rest in the crook of Arthur's shoulder and he had circled his neck with both arms. Maya tried to keep a clear voice as butterflies flew in her stomach at the image.

"I hope he enjoyed the day."

"I'm sure he did."

Arthur gently sat the sleepy child on his bed, while Maya took his pyjamas and started undressing him. The parental gestures came so naturally to both of them that neither really noticed until Matthew was curled in his bed and Maya tugged the sheets around him, kissing his forehead softly.

The young man failed to find some stupid comment to break the spell. She was watching the dark head quietly nestled on the pillow and Arthur gulped. All he wanted was to wrap his arms around her and hold her. At the same time, he knew he had to walk away now, before it was too late. If he stayed, none of them would recover from the fall.

Arthur buried his feelings deep inside and stepped back. He spoke low, partly not to disturb the boy, partly because he didn't trust his voice to stay firm.

"I have to go, Maya. Tristan or Colin will take you home."

Surprised, she lifted her eyes to him and he nearly drowned in the liquid waters. Arthur repeated "I have to go," but he didn't move.

Maya glanced back at her charge without a word and he walked to the door. Of course he paused there, fighting not to turn for one last glance.

"Haven't you forgotten something?"

And he looked. Her playful smile rang warning bells in his head. She had said that once, when she wanted him to kiss her. He hesitated a little too long immobile by the door, and her smile faded. Arthur hated himself for causing the gloom on her beautiful face. Maya turned her attention back to the child again.

"Good night, then. Please tell Tristan I'm here on your way out."

Cutting the strings before they acted on them for good was best. However, his pride bested his good sense at the cold dismissal. Arthur approached the woman seated on the bed. Only the renewed hope in her eyes stopped him from covering her mouth with his. With one last effort of will, he settled for a quick hug and walked out, this time without stopping.

SECOND CHANCES

Chapter 25

Maya saw the papers piled up on her desk and turned tail. She wanted to see Matthew; the paperwork would wait.

The little boy was drawing when she entered the playroom, installed at a small table with colored crayons spread in front of him. He looked pale when she approached; his bright eyes, so much like her own, shone unhealthily. Maya's heart squeezed painfully in her chest. The previous day had left its mark on the fragile child. She walked swiftly to sit near him and hugged him tenderly.

Matthew accepted the caress before he escaped her arms to present her with his drawing. It showed three characters more or less well formed, the smallest one being perched on a big four-legged animal, a horse of course. The horse was so tall it nearly touched the sun in the corner of the sheet. The other two were holding hands, and she recognized herself and Arthur at once. The short yellow hair and long black hair were unmistakable. She caressed his head gently.

"Arthur is working today, Matthew. Maybe he'll come by later."

She wondered if he would. He seemed as attached to the boy as she was, however Matthew and she came as a package deal Arthur was not ready to consider. She wished she could find words to explain that to the small boy. The picture danced in front of her eyes. Matthew's wish was not about riding horses – not really. What he really wanted was a family and to be loved. Chasing away the threatening tears, she stood.

"Gavin told me they are about to show the *'Toy Story'* movie; do you want to come with me and watch it?"

SECOND CHANCES

The dark head nodded up and down, and the slight movement brought a painful cough. Maya rubbed his little back slowly until the child calmed down. The operation was scheduled to happen in less than five days; it seemed too far away. His lips were nearly blue with the need for air.

When his breath finally settled into heartbreaking hisses, she watched carefully as he pushed away from the table, and took her hand to move toward the video room.

*

After lunch, however, she had no choice but to face the monstrous administrative task waiting for her in her office.

The Vallon Hospital tree had just added to her daily paperwork, which in itself was not a surprise; it usually did. And usually, she didn't mind, but today the joyful memories the extra work brought were downcast by Arthur's odd behavior. As if Matthew's health had not been enough to depress her.

His attitude pained and pleased her at the same time, which was all the more confusing. She felt betrayed he hadn't acted on their obvious mutual attraction (even *he* could not deny it) and she admired the fact he kept his word about behaving honorably. Her pride was bruised and his gallantry suited her. Maya couldn't quite decide which feeling was stronger, respect or annoyance. The mountain of work only added to the frustration. Maybe vanity was winning. A little bit.

One minute he was letting his true self (what she wanted to believe was *really* him) show, flirty, generous and kind, and the next, he closed up tighter than an oyster around its pearl.

Maya picked up the first bunch of papers to put some order in the chaos. Had she done something wrong?

170

The first sheet she read was the list of lost items; she put it away to give to her assistant to type and file. She didn't push or pursue him and did her best to accept Arthur the way he was.

The following items were the external guests and the patient lists. She discarded them for filing as well. Why was he running hot and cold like that? If he didn't want her, why had he kissed her back? Unless it'd been just a reflex.

Her heart swelled heavily and her fingers folded the receipt she held. That was it. He didn't share her interest and he didn't know how to tell her. She had mistaken their charade and blossoming friendship for real feelings and foolishly acted on a mirage.

Shame burned her cheeks. She'd been so stupid. She was not Arthur's type; he had made that clear from the beginning.

Maya forced her fingers to unclench and smoothed the thin paper she had crushed. She had to stop it now. The moment was perfect for a breakup anyway. Robert believed they were deeply involved; Matthew's operation was paid and scheduled; a split-up during the Christmas holiday was said to be terrible. She had a rather accurate idea why.

"Just a fake," Maya chastised herself out loud. "It wasn't real."

She focused on her filing again. Work was an excellent remedy for a lonely soul. Arthur was the best proof of that. Her eyes burned a little.

"Hello?"

Maya lifted her head as Isobel entered her office. Her friend instantly noticed her mood.

"What's wrong?"

The raven-haired woman pushed her braid away, swallowing the unwanted tears.

"Nothing. The paperwork is monstrous."

Isobel peeked at the files on her desk.

"I bet. Can I help?"

"Thanks but I'll get through it; I just need to get down to it."

"So work is not why you look so upset. Is it Arthur?"

"What? No, of course not."

Isobel glared; she was too sharp to miss the lie. Maya shook her head to add to the denying. *So much for announcing they were to* 'break up'. She felt her eyes were watering again and looked away.

Sensing the subject was touchy, Isobel didn't insist. She picked up a receipt from the top of one pile.

"What's this? Wow, that much for cupcakes and little sandwiches?"

"What do you mean?"

Maya took the piece of paper back from the other woman. The receipt read $14,000, way too high compared to...

"That's certainly a mistake, I've got the original submission here."

She fished the contract from another file. The total was around $1,400, which was far more logical for an 80-person buffet at a children's party.

"That's certainly fourteen hundred not fourteen thousand; the decimal point is hard to read."

As she said so, Maya examined the receipt closely. It was not that the point was hard to read, it was absent altogether. She grabbed her phone and dialed the caterer's number.

"Good day, Mrs. Nelson, this is Maya Finnegan from the Vallon Hospital... Yes, thank you, it went well. However, I have your receipt here and I think there's a mistake, it reads fourteen thousand... Oh... Of course... No, that's fine, she probably forgot to tell me... Yes, thank you... Bye."

Maya hung up and glanced at Isobel.

"Moira paid the bill in cash and she told them the extra money was an advance for future services."

Her friend raised an eyebrow.

"I've never heard of such a thing."

"Me neither. And I had told Moira I wanted to change the catering services because I had a lot of problems with them while organizing the last event."

This time, Isobel frowned.

"She must have forgotten that. Your sister looked very distracted yesterday."

Maya recalled her sister's behavior with a growing displeasure, from her apparent headache to her passivity as her fiancé... Distracted was a tactful euphemism.

"I don't understand. She has never done such a thing before. Why did she pay cash? Usually we do a check. And where did she find it? Fourteen thousand, that's a lot! With the Foundation's account still frozen, it's not like we can afford to make advances of the sort."

"You have to ask her."

The young woman shook her head, defeated.

"She's not here. She and Cedric took a couple of days off to plan the wedding."

Isobel gave a pensive pout.

"Maya, if you need the money, you should try to recover it, especially if you're not satisfied with the caterer's services. Why don't you talk to Arthur? He's a business lawyer, he can help."

Asking a Pendleton, even Arthur, to interfere with the Foundation was definitely not a good idea. Especially if...

"I don't want to bother him."

Isobel laughed heartily.

"Honey, from what I saw yesterday, he's just waiting for the opportunity to pose as your white knight in shining armor."

"I don't think so."

Even murmured under her breath, Isobel heard the comment and giggled even more.

"Men are men, Maya, Arthur is no better. They need a little push in the right direction from time to time, and they like nothing more than showing off."

Maya pouted at the statement.

"Tristan is not like that."

Her friend grinned widely.

"Nope. But he's mine now and you're stuck with Arthur, who defines the gender. Pamper his pride a bit and ask for his advice. I guarantee pleasant results."

The blonde winked. Maya felt crimson coming up her neck again, as the internal battle raged. Arthur definitely did not require an ego-boost but she needed his expertise. She sighed.

"You're right. I'll talk to him." *'Among other things…'*
"You didn't tell me why you're here."

"Oh, that."

Isobel settled in the chair facing the desk and smiled beautifully.

"I'm relocating to the city, and I plan to be the best Ambassador the Vallon Hospital has ever had. I have the looks, the skills and the connections. So, am I hired?"

Chapter 26

Arthur put his pen down to give the toy car on his desk a small push. The firefighter truck rolled to bump into the phone with a small 'thump'.

'What's that noise? Arthur, are you listening?'

The young man grimaced.

"Sorry, Father, I lost my pen inadvertently."

'Pay attention. I don't care about repeating myself. Paragraph two, line four…'

Arthur sighed discreetly. Robert had been on the phone for most of the afternoon, dictating changes or comments for every single element of the Mercia contract. The monotonous sound was pounding in his head for so long he barely acknowledged the pain; he couldn't remember not feeling it.

'Line five…'

He scribbled a note about rephrasing, which he was pretty sure he would not be able to decipher later. The litany of paragraphs, lines, words was infinite. They turned a page, and Arthur noticed they had only three more to go. The realization came like a light at the end of a tunnel; with any luck, he would be out before seven, and able to catch a complete program on TV before falling asleep from exhaustion.

Colin poked his head through the opening of the door, and Arthur gestured him to go, impatiently.

'Third paragraph, line two…'

That was good. They were in the middle of one page already, which meant only two and half to go, if he could focus for another hour…

Maya entered the room and closed the door behind her back, offering a timid smile. His head jerked up instantly.

175

Apparently, Colin had interpreted his sign as an agreement to let her in. For once, he didn't mind the misunderstanding.

"I'll put you on hold for a minute, Father."

Arthur punched one button without waiting and stood up.

"To what do I owe the pleasure?"

The formal address contrasted with the welcoming sapphire stare he fixed on her; Maya fidgeted a little, playing with her scarf.

"I wanted to ask you something but you're busy so…"

"If you don't mind waiting, I should be done soon. Please sit down."

Arthur showed her to the seat in front of his desk and sat back in his chair, putting his father back on line.

"I'm here, father, please go on."

'Take your time, Arthur, after all, it's only an eight hundred and seventy thousand dollar contract.'

The sarcasm made her frown. Maya glanced up, looking for a reaction from Arthur, but he had just picked up his pen again. Sensing her stare on him, the young man brought one finger to his lips in the eternal 'keep quiet' gesture. His accepting attitude concerned her but she obeyed and kept her mouth shut.

"You were on the… third paragraph."

'Line two, add…'

With Maya quietly settled in front of him, he found it easier to listen to the voice of his father. He looked forward to being alone with her, despite the inevitable torture repressing his feelings would bring him. Arthur concentrated on his notes and ignored the growing tiredness that the implacable tone was raising.

Maya looked around her, curious. She had never been in Arthur's office before and she tried to take in the atmosphere of his daily surroundings. The room was spacious, with wood and leather furniture. The halogen light made it difficult to know what color the cases were, black cherry or dark brown most likely.

The chairs were massive, and the effect with the ultra modern desk of steel and glass was unsettling. Maya decided the overall impression was one of a patchwork of commodities, rather than a carefully chosen décor.

The room looked exactly like the image Arthur wanted to present: a shell, devoid of emotions. It saddened her to realize he walked in here every day without finding a shelter. She was pretty sure if she visited his apartment, it would be the same, both practical and empty.

Maya returned her attention to the desk and saw the toy cars she had offered him. She smiled. He had added a personal touch after all. Pushing on her feet, she circled the desk to give the yellow race car a small push so it rolled over his papers. Arthur looked up and her stomach made that funny loop it did so often when he was close, and she wanted him even closer.

The young man pointed at the phone, indicating her to return to her seat; the temptation was too strong and Maya refused to move away; instead, she began to brush his temples as she had done once to calm his headache. Arthur closed his eyes automatically, giving in to the caress without thinking. The fruity scent from her hair swarmed over him when she bent to touch his forehead. The pulsing in his head was still painful but decreased slowly under her ministrations.

The distorted voice of his father brought him back to reality; Arthur pushed her away firmly, fishing out his lost pen to write another note.

"I hear you Father; is that the last one?"

'For now. I'll meet with them at lunch tomorrow. Send your corrections before ten-thirty.'

The click forbade the young man to protest. He didn't mind the abrupt ending. He knew from experience arguing would have been fruitless. At least his father had saved him from himself.

Maya sat on the desk, balancing her legs in front of her.

"Is he always so hard on you?"

"You know him; business is business."

"You're his only son Arthur, he should…"

Maya stopped talking. Voicing out loud how bad his father treated him was probably the last thing Arthur needed. She could tell he was tired. The slight frown she associated with his recurring headaches was still visible. She wished she could take some of his worries off his shoulders.

She wore slacks instead of a skirt yet the movement of her legs was fascinating. Arthur pinched the ridge of his nose to ease the pressure inside his skull, trying to focus on something other than her body within his reach.

"You had something to ask me?"

The balancing stopped, thankfully.

"Yes, but I'm hungry, and I can't discuss anything seriously when I need food."

Serious conversation sounded no good. Arthur nearly groaned. Maya jumped to her feet.

"Take me to dinner, and I'll tell you everything."

Her engaging smile was something else; and having skipped lunch, he realized he was hungry too.

"Of course. Give me five minutes to make a copy of this for Colin."

*

SECOND CHANCES

The Italian restaurant was nearly full. Apparently, running the sales on Boxing Day excited spirits as well as appetite and they slalomed between tables to reach theirs. Arthur conversed quickly in Italian with their waiter and the man left coming back minutes later with bread-sticks and carbonated water.

"I ordered, I hope you don't mind."

Maya nibbled at one of the grissini; her companion had relaxed the moment they had climbed in his car, and now he seemed (nearly) at ease. She guessed the migraine was almost just a memory. He was quiet, which was his fashion, and it suited her just fine.

"I really like this place."

She did. From peaceful the other night to happily noisy today, the little restaurant had a cheerful exuberance she enjoyed very much. She wondered how it was on Valentine's Day, and Easter, or during the summer, when customers could use the terrace outside.

"So, what's the matter?"

Arthur asked because he had to, not really interested in the answer. Being serious might mean she had noticed how often he overstepped the limits of their 'arrangement' and she wanted him to stop. Or she had talked to Tristan and she wanted to know what was what. Or…

"Isobel said you…"

She trailed off and blushed. Arthur felt his ears warm in turn. Whatever Isobel had suggested could only mean trouble. Oblivious to his embarrassment, Maya went on.

"You see, Moira made a mistake and I was wondering…"

Their plates arrived and he used the diversion to fully compose himself. Maya was still talking.

"With the Foundation's account closed, we can't afford…"

"If you need money, I can…"

"No! No, thank you."

Maya squeezed his hand gently and Arthur lost track of the conversation again. It felt strange to move away from her touch to pick up his fork.

"I don't know what to do…"

Abashed, he glanced up from his ravioli to see her adorable mouth pouting. Looking down again with some difficulty, Arthur settled for a quick questioning, given he had missed half of her explanation.

"Moira overpaid your supplier."

"Yes, for future services."

"Was it included in your contract?"

"No. And I had told her I wanted to change in the future but she…"

"I think you should simply ask for a refund."

Maya smiled beautifully and his chest swelled with pride, then her expression faded.

"She paid cash, it's not going to be a problem is it?"

Step-by-step, pieces of the puzzle he was trying so hard to ignore started to fall into place. Cedric (God, he hated that sneaky bastard) was back from a 'business' trip and suddenly, Moira was 'distracted'… Flying high was more like it. Moira overpaid a Vallon Hospital subcontractor in cash, exceeding the original bill with some random excuse. The supplier had given a receipt, Maya asked for a reimbursement and the cat was in the bag. The process was the perfect plan to launder dirty money. If they could link the cash to the drug dealing… Hell.

Arthur pushed his plate away, his appetite lost.

"Please excuse me."

He stood and walked to the washroom. Now he was trapped between her and his duty. He could forget about it, enjoy their dinner and just let it go. Except...

Hating himself, Arthur picked up the phone.

SECOND CHANCES

Chapter 27

Tristan put down the phone and walked to sit back on the bed. Isobel circled his bare shoulders with both arms to press her cheek against his. Sensing his trouble, she asked softly, "What's the matter?"

The young man covered her hands with his.

"It was Arthur."

Isobel instantly stopped nuzzling his ear and forced him to turn.

"Why did he call you? Is it Maya? What's wrong?"

"Why do you think there's something wrong with Maya?"

Facing him, she touched the small frown between his eyebrows to smooth it.

"You are hardly Arthur's best friend. Maya is your only common interest and she looked very sad this morning."

"She did?"

The worry in his voice was unmistakable. Tristan still didn't like the idea of Maya being one of Arthur's *interests*. However, it was not his choice to make.

"Yes. I'm pretty sure it was related to Arthur, but I didn't prod."

Tristan growled.

"They are having dinner."

Isobel grinned happily, though she hardly believed Arthur was calling Tristan to tell him he was taking his cousin out.

The young man let her pull him back on the mattress, while his mind processed Arthur's call. He had asked if he had received the financial records. He believed Cedric was the mastermind behind the whole problem because Maya had inadvertently given away how the Foundation was used to launder the money. Arthur wanted it to stop; for Maya's sake.

Isobel looked at her silent lover from under her lashes, her chin on his chest. Her intelligent gray eyes sparkled with mischief.

"She's pregnant and she told him, and Arthur called to assure you he is going to make her an honest woman."

Her theory was so far-fetched Tristan chuckled in spite of his worries.

"You're crazy."

"Only about you." She frowned. "He didn't break up with her, did he?"

"No, he didn't."

'Not by a long shot.'

"Good, because Arthur…"

Tristan cupped her neck to drag her closer. He had yet to receive that report and Arthur's big scheme would have to wait until morning. Surely Maya could handle him by herself a bit longer…

"Enough with Arthur…"

*

Maya watched while the restaurant emptied. Attempts at conversation had died due to half-hearted, evasive replies from her companion. Their comfortable zone had gone with Arthur's sudden disappearance during the main course, and it had not come back.

When he moved away as she leaned forward to pick up her glass, Maya had enough.

"Do you mind asking for the bill? I would like to go home."

Her flat tone seemed to shake him. Arthur straightened up in his chair to gesture to their waiter, visibly waiting for an explanation.

Maya considered her options and finally decided honesty was best.

"Let's face it, Arthur, we don't have anything in common beside Matthew. It's okay, we don't have to force ourselves when our friends and family are not around. And if your father is convinced, then…"

She concluded her sentence with a flip of her hand. Offering him a way out was one of the hardest things she had ever done. But seeing him so ill at ease and out of her reach was too much for her to handle. The blue eyes were fixed on her now, as hard to read as ever, and she did her best to bravely hold his stare.

The waiter came back before Arthur had found an answer to demolish her logic. Denial was pointless. They were as close as night and day.

She held her hair up so it didn't get caught in her collar when their host helped her with her coat. She was beautiful, inside and out, and he was attracted to her like a moth to a flame. It was best to put some distance between them. Except that he simply couldn't.

Maya picked up her scarf, a flow of silken hair cascading again, and he took the cloth out of her hands to arrange it himself. Maya bent her head to follow his moves, but Arthur forced her chin up.

"I feel good when you're around and that's enough for me."

Her eyes widened a little, but he didn't wait for a reply and took her arm to escort her outside. He was unlocking her door when Maya murmured,

"That's enough for me too."

Then she climbed in, leaving him speechless on the sidewalk.

They made it as far as the first light before they leaned toward each other and kissed. Arthur managed to move away from her when the light turned green, but they kissed again at the next stop, a short (too long) two hundred feet away, and again two lights later.

The light traffic kept them apart for another thirty blocks, so the impatient honk from a car behind that interrupted their fourth kiss felt like a bombshell. Five stops later, they finally parked in front of Maya's apartment.

Arthur cut off the engine. The latest part of the ride had helped clear his head a little, and doubts started assaulting him once more.

"We're too old to neck in a car like teenagers."

Maya moistened her lips in anticipation and his stare instantly sank to her mouth in spite of his resolve.

"Says who?"

Her permission didn't unleash the passion she was craving. His hands cupped her face, brushing her jaw, seeking answers in the smoky green of her eyes. When his mouth touched hers again, the touch was tantalizing light and soft, before his self-control exploded and he invaded her mouth for a deep passionate kiss. Maya whimpered softly inside his mouth. Or maybe the sound of pleasure was his; they were so lost in each other, it was hard to tell.

Maya circled his neck then moved to caress his chest. His body under her palms was wonderfully strong and hot; definitely not close enough. She leaned closer and the gesture tightened her seat-belt. Shaken, Arthur straightened up, trying to catch his breath.

"What are we doing?"

The windows were already fogging up from the heat rising between them. She smiled impishly.

"You kissed me, and I kissed you back."

Maya touched his face, trying to have his attention again. Arthur swallowed.

"It's not a good idea."

She could feel the restrain in the clench of his jaw under her fingertips and she wanted his willpower gone.

"I don't care."

The caress was bewitching and he closed his eyes to savor the touch. He only had to lean forward to taste her again… Arthur resisted, though he didn't know how.

"I do."

Maya pouted as he gently untied her hands from his neck. "But…"

Arthur leaned back fully in his seat, looking at the crystallization that slowly invaded the windshield. He forced coldness into his voice, for it was the only way to save them both.

"I'm not the right person for you."

His about-face was so complete she briefly wondered if she was dreaming.

Arthur kept his head straight, avoiding her eyes. The pain in his fingers from gripping the wheel so tight was nothing compared to the hole drilling inside his chest. He added arrogance to the next words, hoping her anger would overcome the pain he was inflicting on her.

"You'll thank me later. Trust me."

"You're unbelievable."

Oh, yes, she was angry.

"What's not right is denying who you are or what you want, Arthur."

He wanted her. He wanted a future with her; a family, kids. He wanted to look forward to coming home every night and to have her by his side when he woke up in the morning.

"I can't. I'm sorry."

Maya opened her door and stepped outside the car.

"So am I. Colin will let you know how Matthew is doing."

Game over.

The door banged and he counted down from twenty before he allowed his head to turn, catching the last glimpse of her proud figure entering her home. Within a minute, a light shone through a window. Arthur bent down, started the engine and drove away.

She deserved more than he had to give. The only thing he could offer was to rid the Vallon Hospital and the Foundation of their plague. He turned left toward the office and opened his window wide. The chilly air seemed nearly warm compared to the cold inside his heart.

Chapter 28

"Colin!"

The young man sighed and grabbed the last printed corrections to answer his irascible boss. Whatever had happened after he had let Maya into Arthur's office the previous evening had turned him into a younger version of…

"COLIN!!"

…his father. Entering the room, Colin noticed once again the bloodshot eyes and wrinkled shirt and wondered.

"Thanks."

At least Arthur managed to stay polite in spite of his obvious disarray.

"I nearly waited."

This time, the sarcasm hit a nerve and instead of retreating to the door, Colin glared.

"What happened yesterday?"

"Nothing."

Colin folded his arms over his chest, unmoved by the snap and asked again, adding specifics, "What happened *with Maya* yesterday?"

"None of your business."

Arthur glanced up and recognized the look immediately. Colin was in his *'I'm-not-taking-no-for-an-answer'* mode. His friend was the sweetest man he knew, but he could stand his ground when he wanted to. Like now.

"We went out to dinner, I drove Maya home and then I came back here to work. Where is…"

"Did you fight during dinner, or later?"

Oh, yeah, Colin could be as stubborn as a mule. Arthur lied.

"We didn't fight."

'We kissed. We kissed and I had a glimpse of paradise and I can not have it.'

"Oh boy."

Colin fell into the chair facing the desk.

"You chickened out."

Arthur snorted.

"I certainly did not 'chicken out'. We both decided it was best not to pursue our 'arrangement' any longer."

"Bullshit, Arthur. You're in love with her and, as usual, when you have to take an emotional risk, you backed out."

This one hit home. Arthur narrowed his eyes on his friend, menacingly.

"You have no idea what you're talking about."

Colin glared back, with another of his 'I-know-better' looks and stood.

"I'm going to the Vallon Hospital. You, you are going home to shower, and eat something more nutritious than black coffee. And when you crash in your lonely bed, pray Maya has more good sense than you do."

And a bottomless forgiving heart. He didn't add that part. The gleam in Arthur's eyes was too close to despair for that.

*

The woman pacing back and forth and fuming was not the one he had expected to find.

"Isobel..."

Maya was curled in her chair, and the soft plea stopped the blonde in her furious tracks. She came near her friend swiftly and threw her arms around her to comfort her.

190

"Oh honey, I'm so sorry… I should not have encouraged you to consider him… I knew from the beginning your pairing was a fake, but you seemed so taken with each other…"

The green eyes began to water, despite Maya's resolve not to cry over something that had never been there. She spotted Colin above her friend's shoulder, and pushed away, welcoming him with a tight smile.

"Hi, Colin."

Isobel spun on her heels and narrowed her eyes suspiciously, half-sure Arthur would be right behind his friend. Unimpressed, Colin came near Maya to kiss her cheek then settled in the chair facing her.

"Arthur is an idiot."

The blonde woman approved, ready to start her rant again, but Maya squeezed her hand and she kept her mouth shut.

"Did he tell you…"

She trailed off, unwilling to announce out loud a split that was not really one. It would have made it too real. Colin sighed.

"It wasn't hard to guess. I see him with this air on him only once a year."

'On his birthday, when he comes back from the cemetery… Except this year because he came back to you.'

Maya looked away. Colin searched for the best way to explain without hurting her further (and without being hit by Isobel).

"He is scared, Maya. All he's loved, he has always lost."

Colin took her little nod for an encouragement to speak further.

"Arthur lost his mother, and his father shows no mercy, let alone love for him. And this thing about the Foundation, he is sure it will be his fault if anything bad happens. So he keeps you at arm's length because he thinks it's best for you, whatever the sacrifice costs him. He really cares, Maya."

The young woman stayed mute, maybe thinking about his explanation. She had turned to look through the window. Isobel sneered.

"So what do you suggest, Colin? That she jumps him to force him to overcome his complexes?"

"Well…"

From Colin's point of view, the idea had its appeal. It would certainly lighten his days, that was for sure.

"I can't do that."

Colin sighed again. *It'd been worth a try…*

"Whatever feelings Arthur has for me, they are clearly not strong enough for him to act on them. I will not hurt him intentionally but he'll never be happy if he refuses to risk that I could. It is his choice to make; not mine."

*

Two hours and three cold showers later, the young man still paced his living room like a caged lion. He had considered going to her at least a thousand times, and found as many reasons not to go.

He didn't even try to sleep. The light in her eyes when she had walked away was keeping his exhausted brain awake.

Housework didn't help either. There was not much to do anyway, a couple of cups to gather, one plate in the sink. After ten minutes, he had stopped the dishwasher. The tidal noise was only enhancing those pictures of her he desperately tried to chase from his head, peaceful walks on the beach and her cheeks made pink by pleasure while she moved under him.

SECOND CHANCES

Arthur picked up a glass but the piece escaped his distracted fingers to crash on the floor. The broom soon became a weapon, grabbed with both hands like a sword, and whirling in front of him rather than sweeping the floor.

Years of watching epic movies and training were imprinted in his muscles and he swung the head forward with full force, again and again, each furious movement unfortunately adding to his restlessness. He couldn't stop moving or he thought he would scream.

When the doorbell rang, he was breathless.

For a second, Arthur imagined it was her, that Colin had somehow convinced her to forgive him and that she had come to him. Then good sense kicked in to calm his racing heart. She would never do that, especially after he had walked away so carelessly.

The bell rang again. Arthur moved to the door and found Tristan on his doorstep.

The dark man narrowed his eyes dangerously, peeking at the broom and Arthur's disheveled attire. He looked furious. So Maya had called her cousin to the rescue to punish him. Great. Arthur braced himself for the coming punch. He was stronger than Tristan, but…

His unexpected visitor said nothing though he inhaled deeply, as if to ready himself. Tristan plunged one hand into a pocket and Arthur backed away quickly. Surely he wouldn't…

The other man frowned.

"What's the matter with you?"

Arthur shook his head, appalled. If he was not here to shoot him, then what? He barked:

"What do you want?"

Tristan glared. Arthur glowered back. He didn't care. The truce between them had shattered the moment he had started to believe Maya could mend his soul.

Tristan shoved a flash drive in his hand.

"You need to see that."

Fantasies about Maya definitely vanished from Arthur's head when he opened the files on the disk.

Chapter 29

Maya examined her face in the mirror. Despite her firm refusal, not running to Arthur was hard. She already knew what Colin had said, more or less, and she ached to take him in her arms and lighten his burden; to make him feel loved and whole again. She knew she could. But he had to trust her with his heart, unconditionally, or neither would be happy.

She turned the hot water on. Sleep had eluded her a good part of the night before, and she hoped a long bath would help chase the sad edginess away and relax her.

It didn't take long to fill the tub, and Maya lowered herself into the water with a soft sigh of contentment. The heat blazed her skin instantly and she stayed still in the bath for a while, enjoying the sensation and the slight dizziness invading her head. While stretching to grab her soap, the water around her rippled in hot gentle waves. The salts she had added created a fragrant film on her skin and Maya rubbed her hands on her arms and her calves, savoring the caress.

Arthur's image was still in the back of her mind, but she felt calmer now. The pain his attitude had caused seemed enclosed in a thick cloud she hoped was oblivion. In a couple of weeks, when she'd forgotten about the sparks between them, she would call him and allow him around her and Matthew again, as a *friend*.

She forgot about the soap to enjoy the hot liquid, playing her fingertips on the fragile liquid surface, then moving her open palms into the water like a dolphin, with a childish grin.

The doorbell broke through her bubble. She guessed Isobel was coming to the rescue again, probably with Tristan this time, and as much as she loved them, she wanted to be left alone. Closing her eyes, Maya refused to acknowledge the disturbance.

The bell rang again, twice, and this time she couldn't ignore it. She rose from the water with a heavy sigh and draped her robe around her, then lifted the plug to empty her tub. She had little chance of getting rid of the importunate visitors and coming back to her bath before it cooled completely.

Tristan was indeed waiting on her doorstep. Her eyes, however, rested on the blond figure by his side.

Arthur fisted his hands deep in his pockets to prevent them from reaching for her. A delicate scent was drifting from her, intoxicating. Some wet tendrils had escaped from her loose bun to caress her slender neck and her porcelain skin was pink, maybe from water that was too hot. She was clutching the belt of her robe while her vivid eyes searched his face. He swallowed hard. She was the most desirable thing he had ever seen.

Tristan stepped forward, but she stayed stiff in her cousin's embrace, her eyes never straying from Arthur.

"Maya, we need to talk to you."

Arthur was grateful Tristan took the initiative. His tongue was glued to his palate, his mouth parched, and all he could think was to fall on his knees and beg.

She turned away silently to invite them in, and the spell lifted partly, allowing him to breathe again.

"Give me a minute."

The young woman escaped to her room to dress. Tristan turned toward Arthur who was still frozen near the door.

"Maybe it's better if I explain."

He never felt that clumsy in front of anyone. Arthur suspected his sudden capacity to use words came from her exiting the room. He choked a vague "Be my guest," before language eluded him again.

Maya leaned against the closed door, shaken. She had seen him less then 24 hours ago, and he looked taller, broader, his eyes bluer, his whole being echoing into her to make her heart race. He looked more tired, too, and troubled. She couldn't fathom why he was there with Tristan; her cousin was more likely to kill Arthur for being such a jerk rather than try to bring them together. At least she thought he was.

The young woman put on jeans and a sweater, before she took a deep breath and joined her unexpected visitors in the living room.

*

Their drinks stayed untouched on the coffee table. Only Maya had hers on her knees, and her hands cupped the hot mug, seeking a sense of reality in their story.

Tristan had taken the lead and related fact after fact about the Foundation and Moira, Cedric, and the drug money. The incredible accusations floated between the three of them and she tried to wrap her mind around them.

She didn't know what hurt the most, her sister being an addict for so long without her even noticing, or Moira turning something good they had created together into a farce. Maybe it had been her intention all along to use the foundation for dirty business. Suddenly, it all made sense: the changing moods, the depression when Cedric (her supplier!) was absent, Moira's epic fights with Robert when he tried to control her. Her godfather had been the only one who had actually _done_ something to stop it. If he had confided in her, instead of treating her like a baby and later pushing her away, she might have been able to help. That was what hurt the most. Not having been granted a chance to help.

Arthur saw the pain flashing in her beautiful eyes, and only that made him decide to speak.

"I should have told you from the beginning what was happening with the Foundation, Edana. I'm sor…"

"Don't you dare call me that."

Pain lost the battle against cold rage. She stood to face him, her cheeks colored in anger.

"You lied to me and you used me even after I…"

Her voice was high-pitched and she paused a second.

"Not once. Not once did you try to tell me the truth. You promised me you'd treat me decently. You broke your word."

Maya was about to add he was no better than his father, but shut up. She was mad, but not enough to hurt him intentionally. Not yet.

Tristan had noticed his companion's posture hardening with each accusation. However, Maya's wrath was more of a concern to him. Her stare had paled to the color of pale jade. Sensing the danger, he interfered.

"Arthur came to me, Maya. It was our decision to…"

"Don't."

Arthur interrupted him; he couldn't let someone else take the blame for his mistakes.

"Maya, Tristan advised me to tell you and also to break our deal, and I didn't."

He stood up.

"We have insufficient proof, but it might be enough to obtain an injunction for a legal investigation. You deserved to know it before seeing your sister under arrest, or the police probing through your files. Please accept my apology."

The calming effect from her bath seemed centuries away. Maya sat back in her seat, ignoring Arthur and avoiding her cousin's stare. Tristan too was pushing to his feet when her question resounded in the room.

"What would be considered sufficient proof?"

Arthur turned toward her. This time she held his stare firmly.

"Cedric and Moira can be linked to cash flows which are not related to the usual operations of the Foundation. But there's nothing to prove Cedric deals drugs."

She gave it a thought. "Yes, there is."

Her assurance surprised both men.

"I saw him giving Moira some pills on Christmas Day. She claimed she had a headache."

Recognition lit Arthur's eyes. "When I found you in her office…"

The memory also awoke the protective beast in his chest. Maya nodded.

"Yes. That's proof, isn't it?"

Triumph glittered in her green stare, but Arthur stayed impassive.

"Circumstantial, again. It could have been aspirin. We can't prove it was not."

"Then we need some of those pills."

Tristan looked grimly at the ping-pong contest between them. He knew his cousin well enough not to try keeping her out of it again. Unfortunately Arthur didn't, and he reacted instantly, fool as he was.

"I don't want you to be involved in this."

Maya frowned and annoyance flared in her eyes so fiercely her opponent nearly stepped back.

"I don't remember requiring your permission."

Piqued, Arthur folded his arms on his chest and smirked.

"And how do you intend to recover the drugs? You think he is graciously going to give it to you?"

"Maybe. But I'll have to ask very nicely."

He caught the lowering in her voice before a shadow dimmed her face swiftly. Then her meaning sank and he roared.

"NO!"

Tristan understood too, his reaction coming less intense but just as stern.

"Absolutely not, Maya."

The young woman stood gracefully and started toward her bedroom. Arthur grabbed her arm and she pulled away with equal force, yet unable to shake him off.

"Get your hands off me."

The order did nothing to calm him. In no way was he allowing her to go to that brute and... He nudged her against the door, uncaring of her gasp when his fingers bit hard into her tender shoulders, or of her cousin being only feet away. His mouth crashed on hers. Her head bumped into the frame and she choked, nearly surprised he didn't use the opportunity to invade her mouth. It shamed her to feel arousal pouring inside her at the aggression.

For a second, he felt her quiver against him, as if she was going to kiss him back, half-hoping she would, but Maya pushed him brutally.

"GET OFF ME!"

Her shout was nearly hysterical. Arthur freed her arms, and smirked nastily.

"You can't stand being touched by someone you dislike. You'll never convince him."

Maya glared down on him.

"I can, and I will."

She smiled at her cousin sweetly, shot another scornful glance to Arthur, and banged the door in both their faces.

SECOND CHANCES

Chapter 30

In a way, she was lucky, Maya thought. It was Friday, which meant Moira was at her yoga class and Cedric was alone at home.

She smoothed her skirt nervously. A double dose of Arthur's abusive behavior and the rightful anger it arose would help right now. She pushed aside the troubling memories of the possessive kiss and squared her shoulders, pushing her chin up proudly. Part of her bravado might have come from some irresistible need to make Arthur pay; she could do this, and would. If she had managed to shove him away, Cedric didn't stand a chance; did he? In addition, the police officer had confirmed it was a good plan.

*

Arthur looked at the inspector in front of them with a very annoyed expression on his face.

"You were supposed to convince her otherwise, Luke, not encourage her."

The man shook his head.

"We've been trying to nail Cedric for months now and he's systematically managed to dodge the traps; this is a perfect opportunity because it could potentially give him the full control of the Finnegan sisters, so hopefully his greed will lower his guard."

Arthur growled. It was not greed that interested the guy but...

Luke went on.

"Miss Finnegan will wear a bug and if she manages to have Cedric admit something compromising, we will have enough material to issue a warrant for his arrest and to search his place."

"This is unacceptable, the risks..."

Her murdering glance shut Arthur up. Then Maya turned to Luke.

"I can't wear a bug under my clothes, he'll notice."

Arthur's disgusted sneer was priceless. She could hear the jealous wheels in his head spinning. The officer answered,

"We'll use your cell phone. You'll only have to call a specific number I'll give you and to keep your phone on, so we'll record everything."

*

Maya resisted turning her head toward her cousin's car down the street. Her phone was open in her pocket and the three men would be hearing her verbal exchanges with Cedric. And if she screamed, it would take them less than a minute to come over. But she would not scream. She would lure Cedric into giving her some of his 'medicine' and talking about his crimes, so his abhorrent trafficking would stop.

Maya placed her best innocent smile on her lips and rang the bell.

*

The man was barefoot and his shirt half-opened when he came to the door. When he saw her, the annoyance on his face changed into a carnal sneer.

"Hey... My delightful baby sister-in-law... It's my lucky day after all... Please, come..."

"Hi Cedric."

The door clapped on her like a mousetrap. Following him inside, Maya put her coat away so she was sure he didn't notice the phone was online.

"I'm sorry to bother you on your vacation... I've got something to ask you... Moira is out so..."

She put enough coyness in her words to catch his interest. She didn't need to play to sound hesitant.

*

Arthur groaned.

"We can't let her do that. The man is a brute, he can't think of anything else but..."

Tristan shot him a dark glare.

"That's the point."

Luke in the backseat said nothing. Arthur growled again; Luke had accepted being involved as a punishment for Arthur stealing Emily from him. Idiot. Arthur tried to forget it was Maya in the house with the bastard.

*

She waited in the living room, unwilling to be out of her phone's reach, while Cedric moved to the kitchen and came back with his coffee. She was glad he didn't offer her one; her stomach was so tense the smell of the strong beverage was enough to disturb her.

Maya presented him with another weak smile and a flutter of lashes when he sat close to her on the couch. "You said I just have to ask… You see, Arthur has those terrible migraines and the pills you gave Moira seemed so efficient…"

*

Even muffled by the fabric of her coat, the tremor in her voice was unmistakable. It came from fear. He knew it did. It galled Arthur even more. He flexed his fingers on his lap, trying to ignore the anger rising in his chest.

Tristan peeked at his companion at the mention of his migraines, but stayed focused on the phone.

*

Cedric's hand brushed her leg when he put his cup down and she bit the inside of her cheek not to jump away. The contact made her twitch, and the man grinned arrogantly. Maya placed one hand on his arm.

"Please, Cedric…"

She hoped he mistook the quivers in her fingers for worry for Arthur, instead of the rising panic it really was. His skin was too hot under her palm, and he was way too close.

*

Hearing her 'please' was unbearable.

Hateful images were playing in his head; the rogue had his hands on her and she was allowing it. He didn't care about exposing the dealer, he didn't care about his father's reaction if he screwed this sole chance up, he didn't care if she never looked at him again; he just could not hear the fear in her voice while she begged.

206

*

The despicable fingers found their way to her knee.

"Those are not free, Babe... They're illegal and I took them in for Moira..."

"Please... I'll repay you, I'll..."

A pair of voracious lips swallowed hers. Maya couldn't help it and stiffened at the contact. Cedric pulled away and laughed.

"What will darling Arthur say when he learns how you paid for his medicine?"

Maya dipped her head so her 'companion' didn't see the disgust and shock in her eyes.

Cedric laughed harder.

*

Tristan's hands clutched the wheel so hard his knuckles had turned white. He could see how the whole scene was affecting Arthur and he was no different.

It was his kin Cedric was harassing. The man was a pig. He had suffered him for Moira but now... He loved Maya like a sister and this... This was madness. He'd never forgive himself if anything... He glared at Luke in the mirror.

"Five more minutes and I'm going, proof or no proof."

Arthur nodded fiercely. Tristan could console Maya while he'd rip the brute apart.

*

Maya used the short retreat of her future brother-in-law to compose herself. If those pills only cost her a few sloppy kisses and venturing hands, she would gladly pay the price to clear her father's Foundation and deliver her sister from the rogue.

Cedric reappeared in front of her with a small envelope, and shirtless. Maya swallowed as he bent forward to put the envelope in her hands.

She couldn't suppress the small gasp when tongue and teeth attacked her jugular. Her nails bit into his chest when his fingers slipped intimately over her knee to reach the hem of her skirt.

*

Arthur grabbed his doorknob, panicked.

"They're not talking, this is not normal. We have to..."

But the two other men had already rushed out of the car.

She was walking swiftly toward them, her head down and her hair flowing around her like a black veil.

Arthur grabbed her shoulders, checking her from head to toe. He noticed at once the mark on her throat and the blood drained from his body.

"What happened? Are you hurt? Did he–"

She was trembling so hard for an instant he thought she was going to collapse in his arms. But Maya just looked up to him, her eyes blazing. He could almost hear her heart pumping shame and anger in her veins.

"He said to come back with money, next time."

Her voice broke, a pallid reflection of his heart splitting in two. She pushed a thick envelope in his hands and turned away to run into her cousin's arms.

Chapter 31

From there, the day went into overdrive. The pills and the verbal recording of Cedric confirming he had imported illegal drugs with the intent to sell them convinced the judge to sign all the warrants.

Moira and Cedric were arrested later in the day and brought into custody. Both tried to blame it on the other, which resulted in a full testimony from the two accomplices.

Maya and Tristan gave their statements and managed to stay out of the media frenzy courtesy of Isobel's skills in keeping the noisiest reporters at bay.

Arthur spent the day trying to unfreeze the Foundation accounts, and return their control into the rightful hands. Working was something he could do by heart. It wasn't difficult. He simply had to fill in forms, throw a few lines on paper, and Colin did the rest, typing letters and adding addresses or names. He referred to the Foundation by a file number or a bank account and discarded names. He worked to avoid thinking, and to escape the black hole inside him that swallowed emotions he didn't know how to deal with. He had not the energy to face it. He was sure if he did, he was going to break.

He was signing the last paperwork when the door of his office opened violently. Robert marched into the room, visibly furious.

"Arthur."

The tone was more cutting than ever and the young man would have winced if he hadn't been emotionally exhausted. He welcomed the intrusion without looking up from his notes.

"Good day, Father. Congratulations are in order, I think."

"Congratulations!?"

The spat exploded in the quiet room.

"You were supposed to retrieve the control of the Foundation for us! What…"

"No."

The denial fired Robert's furor for good and he opened his mouth to vociferate his displeasure but Arthur beat him, standing up.

"My job is to protect the interests of P and A clients, in regard of the law. That's exactly what I did."

"Nonsense. You're not thinking with your head and you let whatever feelings you think you have for that ungrateful little tramp get in the way."

"I told you once, Father, not to insult Maya in front of me. Her only crime was to love and trust her family, which is more than I ever got from you."

Being confronted was something Robert never took well. He moved forward, menacing, but Arthur stood his ground, impassive.

"You'll watch your tongue, Arthur, sarcasm is just good enough for your usual court."

"It's not sarcasm, Father, it's fact. We stopped being a family the day mom died."

He was tired, too tired to pretend any longer.

"Don't you dare speak of my wife to justify your lack of…"

"Your wife was *my* mother! I lost her and I lost you because you had to blame someone for her death!"

"Shut up."

Arthur was far too gone to do so.

"You blame me because she's gone; you tolerate me as long as I bend to your commands, but I stopped being your son long ago."

"I told you to shut up!"

The two men were facing each other, Robert's face was purple with rage while Arthur's was as white as a sheet of paper. He went on nonetheless. He had nothing left to lose, anyway.

"Speaking of Mom, I took a look at her will today. Which…," the young man turned to grab a sheet behind him on his desk, "was very instructive. *I* am her heir, you only had the temporary use of the money. If I'm not mistaken, that makes us equal partners, given you also use *my* money to buy Gerald's shares from Moira and Maya. So, I hold fifty percent of P and A and a right to veto. From now on, I do have to agree to any decision Pendleton & Associates makes. I'm taking back Mom's property. And I'm taking a two-week vacation. These are effective immediately."

He waited for a reply that never came. Robert stayed mute, visibly looking for a fault in Arthur's plan and finding none.

The silence lengthened, hanging heavily above their heads. Arthur felt drained. Keeping exhaustion out of his face was more difficult by the minute. He held his stare up; yielding now would be giving away his soul, in addition to everything else.

"Have the Mercia contract amendments on my desk before you leave, please."

Robert turned around and exited the room.

Arthur crashed on his chair, the papers escaping his hands and falling on his desk. Their landing set the firefighter truck in motion until it rolled off the surface. The young man caught it in midair, and stared at the toy for a second before he put it back on his desk.

His vision blurred and, pressing his fingers to his eyes to clear them, Arthur realized that for the first time in nearly twenty years, he was crying.

*

Maya tried to ignore the gray walls and how they contrasted with the aggressive color of her sister's inmate clothes, which made her look even paler as she sat at the austere table in the visiting room.

Tristan had not been pleased she had decided to visit her sister so soon; they had not argued about it, they rarely did. He had simply pointed out bluntly that he considered Moira as guilty as Cedric, and that he needed time to forgive her. Maya had looked away during the discussion, and stayed quiet.

She wished he'd come with her. Isobel was waiting for her, but it was not the same. Tristan was family, as close as a brother she had never had. Facing both Arthur's desertion and Moira's sedition on her own, without Tristan's support, was hard.

He hadn't wanted to talk about Arthur either, though he gave no particular reason for it. She guessed old discords had resurfaced again within the last 48 hours.

It was just as well. She didn't want to talk about Arthur either. She didn't want to even think about him. He had used her for his own means, from the beginning, and…

Maya shook her head to chase away the upcoming anger and sadness and concentrated on her sister.

Moira had grabbed her hands feverishly, her grip almost painful.

"I'm glad you're here."

Maya gently squeezed her hand back.

"How are you feeling?"

The question was purely rhetorical. The dark eyes were burning from an unnatural fire, the need for a fix all too visible. The fingers under hers trembled and Moira fisted her hand to stop it.

"I'm sorry, Maya. I didn't know what I was doing."

"I know."

The raven-haired woman smiled gently and caressed the fisted hand.

Moira seemed to relax and her face held some resemblance to that of the flamboyant woman she used to be.

"I'll be better as soon as you'll take me out of here. Are we going?"

The old arrogance reverberated in her voice. Maya lowered her eyes and Moira understood. She grasped her sister's wrist in a claw-like grasp, the proud tone changing into a plea.

"You're taking me home, aren't you?"

She felt cold to have to back away from her sister. A part of her had already forgiven her for what she had done. She was not herself then. Maya hesitated then shook her head slowly. "I'm sorry, Moira."

The plea changed into a jeer.

"This is your fault. You tricked my Cedric and you put me here so your precious Pendletons can have what's mine. You were always jealous of me. Thief, liar, bit…"

Maya freed her hand and stood, walking away from the table.

The fury swearing behind her was not her sister. Her sister was the overjoyed woman who applauded and whistled the day she received her diploma; the motherly girl who enfolded her in her arms the first time a boy stood her up; the playful friend who shared her wardrobe every time she had a date and laughed with her for hours about silly things. Her sister was buried somewhere underneath the cruel effects of the drugs. It would take time and patience to win her back.

Maya turned, swallowing her tears.

"I love you, Moira. I'll come back soon."

The door closed on the insults a hateful harpy was shouting at her. Maya ignored them and smiled bravely at Isobel. That witch was not her sister.

Chapter 32

The pounding in his head increased when he moved, the hard blows reverberating from his forehead to the back of his neck. Arthur swallowed, disturbed by the heaviness on his tongue. He remembered one hurtful glance, and the pouring of whisky to drown the ice in his veins.

The messy sheets around him seemed unfamiliar. The waitress had been friendly; maybe too friendly. He straightened up instantly, and the swift movement caused more hammer jabs into his skull. The bedroom was his, however, and he was still fully dressed. He had not even removed his tie or his jacket before passing out. Untying the worn cloth from around his neck to ease his breathing, Arthur wished he could tell it was a good thing.

The floor wobbled under his feet when he stood up. The clock on his bedside table read four a.m. How much had he drunk? More than too much, that was for sure. His head revolted in the upright position.

He remembered more of the past day. The shouting contest with his father; the legal consequences of exposing Cedric, Moira and the drug trafficking. He felt like crap, and so miserable he was ready to cry again. She had looked so aloof… His blurry mind refused to even think of her name.

Arthur bent down to splash some fresh water on his face and vertigo banged through him so hard he had to grip the sink for balance. Draining as much alcohol as he could have seemed quite a brilliant idea the previous night. *Drink to forget until you forget why you're drinking.* Hell of an idea if someone asked him now.

A shrill noise pierced his eardrums and he grunted in pain.

The phone was on the floor in the living room. Maybe it had fallen from his pocket. Maybe he had pitched it; he didn't know; didn't care to remember. Crouching to grab the damn thing sent more waves of dizziness through him.

"Arthur Pendleton... What! ... Of course you have my permission! ... You'd better have started already. If anything happens to this child because of your bureaucratic idiocy, I'll make sure you'll never work in a hospital again. I'll be there in twenty minutes."

Arthur forgot about showering and the hangover; he forgot about his father and about his personal hell. He just grabbed his keys. He was not sober enough to drive. He forgot about that too.

He saw her as soon as he stepped inside the emergency room, Tristan and Isobel were by her side. Her face was hidden in her cousin's neck, and he could tell by the tremors in her shoulders that she was crying or trying very hard not to. Isobel was caressing her back, her hand slowly brushing her hair to appease her. His heart squeezed so hard Arthur hesitated. She hated him; she would not accept him by her side. The need to comfort her, however, overcame his doubts and he stepped forward.

His stare came across Tristan's and he saw the other man's eyes narrowing on him; he murmured something and Maya jolted in her seat, her marvellous green gaze coming to rest on him.

For a second, his heart stopped beating as he watched the tears shining there. And then she was in his arms, seeking comfort in his embrace as if he were the only one who could give it. Arthur brought her closer. His breath stunk from all the alcohol he had drunk. His clothes were wrinkled from a blackout night. He didn't care. He wanted to hold her, to be her champion, to keep deceptions and pain at bay for as long as she would let him.

"I'm sorry."

The tears she was holding back threatened to flow once more when his arms closed around her. His coat was cold and wet from the falling snow, so Maya buried her nose in his shirt instead. He smelled of bars and smoke; the sour scent mixed with the acrid odor of dried sweat. She wanted to fight, to yell, to push him away, and to hit him for all the pain her heart could no longer contain. Maya realized she had started crying when his embrace tightened. She felt so powerless… She needed him desperately.

"I'm sorry, Edana. Please don't cry…"

He trailed off when Maya didn't acknowledge him and continued sobbing silently. She barely heard Tristan explaining the sudden urgency of operating, the tumor in the boy's throat pressing against the trachea and blocking the way to his lungs. Arthur helped her back into her seat. Reasons could wait. All that mattered was the woman in his arms.

"He'll be fine. I know he will."

"You promise?"

The trembling words were so full of anguish, mixed with irrational hope. He wished she hadn't asked that. He could not lie to her, not anymore. Her gaze plunging into his was unbearably bright. It nearly broke his heart again to answer.

"I wish I could."

Her eyes watered again. Maya moved away but Arthur pulled her back to him, one hand cupped around her face, his free arm firmly secured around her. He caressed her wet cheeks gently. Tears were still pearling along the soft lashes, and he dried them one by one until she closed her eyes under the light touch.

They sat in the waiting room, Arthur holding her as closely as he could, and she lost track of time, cradled by the steady beating of his heart against her cheek. At some point, he rested his chin on her head, listening to her calmer breathing and closed his eyes. Maya slipped her arms around his waist to stay warm and fall asleep too.

At six a.m., Tristan and Isobel left, but they promised to stop by again later. Some nurses entered the surgery block and others came out. None talked to them.

At seven a.m., Colin and Gavin showed up with muffins, coffee and a change of clothes for Arthur. He used the employees' quarters to shower and dress, while Colin kept Maya company.

At eight a.m., they were still waiting, no one explaining anything; Arthur lost his temper and Maya calmed him down with a single touch. She thanked the tired attendant with a smile and the woman nodded. She said the doctor would come by soon to answer all their questions. They sat back to wait.

The surgeon showed up forty minutes later. The middle-aged woman pulled off her mask and sighed. Arthur shook Maya gently.

"Are you the parents?"

"I'm Arthur Pendleton, his guardian. Please, tell us how is he doing?"

"The boy is stabilized. He will stay under observation until he wakes then we'll allow him back to his room. Some tests must be run to make sure all the intrusive tissues were removed. Perhaps later this week, if he is strong enough."

"Matthew. His name is Matthew. Not 'the boy'."

The tired woman waved her hand to dismiss Maya's stern comment. She too had had a long night. "Yes. I suggest you go home now, and take a good rest. He won't be allowed visitors until late this afternoon."

Arthur squeezed the surgeon's hand before Maya argued further. "Thank you, Doctor."

The young woman collapsed in his arms. He feared she would start crying again. "I want to see him."

"Soon, Edana. He is resting now."

Arthur tried to loosen his grip on her but he realized he too was shaking. He held her (to her) for what seemed an eternity, before he could feel his heart beating normally again.

"Come with me."

Gavin, who had started his shift, led them toward the south ward where Matthew had his room.

The second bed was still empty. Arthur lay down and pulled Maya to him, her back on his chest, tying his arms around her to link their hands against her chest. Her hair smelled of roses and he bathed in the scent in silence, taking comfort from the softness and the warmth of her body cuddled against his. Her still-labored breathing told him she was not sleeping.

"Why didn't you tell me from the start about the Foundation and Moira?"

Her question threw him off balance. He hadn't expected her to ask about that now. Arthur answered quietly. "You would not have believed me."

The bare truth hung in the air, heavy above them. After a minute, Maya turned on the narrow bed to look at his face. Her eyes were still a little puffy for the crying, but the light in the vivid stare gave him strength to go on.

"When the hospital called me, I panicked. I had to be here with you and Matthew, my only thought was that you needed me. I couldn't think of anything else. I probably ignored a lot of red lights coming."

The joke fell flat; Maya kept searching his face with serious eyes. "I need you to need me too."

"I do."

She considered his answer for a moment before she asked another question, "Do you love me?"

His heart spoke before he did and Maya probably heard it, for she freed one hand from under them, to caress his face gently, his nose and his lips, before she pressed her mouth to his. Her kiss tasted wonderful and Arthur didn't want it to end, but he let her break the contact without a move.

"I love you too."

She nestled back against him, burying her face in his chest like a kitten seeking caresses. The touch unleashed something deep inside him. Love, pain, and need fused together to create a hunger so violent he couldn't or didn't even try to resist. Arthur cupped her neck to pull her face up and he deepened the kiss as soon as their lips touched. Pinning her down on the mattress, he devoured her mouth, her neck, her throat before capturing her lips again when he felt her arch under him.

His hands fisted in her hair became almost painful. The skin of his throat was deliciously hot under her mouth. His heart was hammering against her hand. She briefly wondered why layers of clothes between them were still in her way, stopping her from having more of him to taste. She wanted more.

When he slid one hand under them to find the soft skin of her hip under her blouse, Maya tried to take a hold of him, looking for something solid in the raging feelings his passion was arousing inside her. Her elbow hit the hard rail of the hospital bed when she reached for him. The sharp pain sobered her instantly and a soft moan escaped her. Arthur recoiled instantly misunderstanding her whimper. "Sorry... I'm sorry... We'll take it as slow as you want. I..."

Maya touched his forehead with hers, finally able to circle his chest with both arms. Something was missing, though she was unable to name it just yet.

A dangerous gleam flashed in his stare when the movement crushed her curves deeply into him, but this time he kept the slightest grasp he had on the beast roaring in his blood, the craving laboring his breathing while his fingers hooked onto the tender flesh of her waist. She giggled softly, delighted to know she could shatter his control so easily.

"I'm not a blushing virgin, Arthur. I want to be with you. With. You."

Saying this, her eyes slid toward the empty space beside them and the young man understood instantly. She would answer kisses for kisses, caresses for caresses. But she wanted to give him everything, no holding back, and she couldn't because her heart was still trembling for Matthew. He loved her even more for it. Arthur crushed her into his chest, breathing deeply to calm himself.

"We have time."

A lifetime. He grinned.

"But stop tempting me."

Her playful little pout against his throat nearly bested him.

"And how will I do that?"

Arthur shifted off her and enfolded her in his arms again.

"I have no idea."

Maya closed her eyes and let sleep take her, a content smile on her lips. Arthur stayed awake, guarding her dreams while he waited for the child to come back to them.

Epilogue

Four months later…

The young boy waved happily and her heart skipped a beat. Maya quickly swallowed back her shout for Matthew to keep his hands on the reins. He was so small, perched on the enormous animal.

Something pressed on her back and she had to take one step forward to keep her balance. Arthur's trademark smirk welcomed her when she turned. He was bent forward on his saddle, caressing the neck of the gray horse, and murmuring into its small ears. The animal had soft brown eyes, and if it hadn't been so big, she would have found it adorable. Arthur offered his hand.

"Come on…"

Maya instantly backed off.

"Oh no, no way."

"Come on, she's harmless."

The gray mare whinnied softly.

"You don't have anything to fear, I'll ride with you."

Childish laugher erupted from the paddock where Matthew had switched from walk to trot. She turned toward the paddock, ready to use the child as an excuse. "Matthew is having the time of his life. Leon will show him how to take care of the horse after his lesson. Come on; there's something I want you to see."

He grinned.

"You're not going to let a nine-year-old boy beat you, are you?"

The tease earned the laughing young man a haughty glare, but it worked. "Fine."

Arthur grabbed her wrist and pulled her upward, helping her to settle sideways on the saddle in front of him. "Ready?"

"No."

He laughed some more when Maya fastened her arms around him as the horse started to move. Arthur took both reins in one hand, guiding the horse with his knees. Maya gasped when his free hand slipped around her waist. "Can you keep your hands on the horse?"

"Are you worried?"

"No."

"That makes a lot of 'no'…"

He hurried their pace. She screamed:

"Yes!"

Arthur laughed.

"You need to hear the question first, Edana."

Eyes widened in surprise, she forgot about the horse and turned to meet the smiling blue eyes set on her. Arthur slowed his mount then stopped. They had reached the main house, and the entrance to the library. He jumped down and secured his hands on her hips to help her off the horse.

"See? You didn't fall."

Maya made a face at him and followed him inside. The bay windows were wide open, and the room was filled with the light scent of early flowers and that special smell spring brought to the air. Easter sun rays were dancing in the room. Arthur picked up some papers and a pen on the desk.

"Here. You have to sign this."

"What is it?"

'We, Arthur Pendleton and Maya Finnegan, by affixing our signatures below, do hereby take responsibility of the child

*known as Matthew Wolf. Any and all requirements, including
but not limited to food, clothing...'*

She looked up instantly.

"Arthur, this is..."

She didn't finish her sentence and pulled him to her. His
scent was made of fresh air and of horses, warm and strong and
intoxicating. The papers escaped her hand to land back on the
desk when she lost herself in the kiss. Maya pulled him even
closer, unable to repress a sigh of pleasure. Arthur murmured
against her lips.

"Matthew will need a mother."

"Yes."

"And I need a wife..."

"Yes."

"I want more kids."

"Yes."

"We'll live here."

"Yes."

"You'll wear white at every ball from now on."

"I said yes, Arthur."

"Good."

He kissed her again, and Maya briefly wondered if it was
that bad, that the curtains were wide open and the door
unlocked.

The end is only the beginning
February 2011

www.ingramcontent.com/pod-product-compliance
Lightning Source LLC
Chambersburg PA
CBHW031324170626
46807CB00002B/561